Texas Legacy

Also by Lorraine Heath

TEXAS LEGACY

LORRAINE HEATH

AVONIMPULSE
An Imprint of HarperCollinsPublishers

Excerpt from *Texas Destiny* copyright © 1997 by Jan Nowasky.

TEXAS LEGACY. Copyright © 2019 by Jan Nowasky. All rights reserved. Printed in the United States of America. No part of this book may be used or reproduced in any manner whatsoever without written permission except in the case of brief quotations embodied in critical articles and reviews. For information, address Harper-Collins Publishers, 195 Broadway, New York, NY 10007.

Digital Edition JANUARY 2019 ISBN: 978-0-06-285609-8
Print Edition ISBN: 978-0-06-285610-4

Cover art by Christine M. Ruhnke
Cover photographs © TonyNg/salajandani/Shutterstock (2 images);
© Period images (couple)

Avon Impulse and the Avon Impulse logo are registered trademarks of HarperCollins Publishers in the United States of America.
Avon and HarperCollins are registered trademarks of HarperCollins Publishers in the United States of America and other countries.

FIRST EDITION

19 20 21 22 23   HDC   10 9 8 7 6 5 4 3 2 1

For all the wonderful readers who waited
patiently for twenty years . . .

CHAPTER ONE

August 1909

The telegram found him in Cheyenne, the words simple and to the point: *I need you home. Love, Ma.*

He'd ridden out to the ranch where he'd been working as foreman, given his notice, packed up his few meager belongings, hightailed it to the railway depot, and hopped on the first train going through that would get him to where he needed to be as quickly as possible. Leighton, Texas, a town once described as being on the far side of nowhere, but when he'd left, had been bustling with activity and promise. The railroad had changed its destiny.

No, that wasn't quite right, he mused as he sat beside a window on the lumbering train and watched the empty vastness rolling by. Dallas Leigh had created the town from nothing, courted the railroad barons to ensure a stretch of track went through his town to increase its chances of thriving, and in so doing had altered the makeup of the land and the lives of a good many people. He, along with his wife, had changed Rawley Cooper's life as well, had dragged him from the hellhole that had been his boyhood existence and given him more opportunities than he deserved. Which was the reason Rawley hadn't hesitated to leave everything behind when he received the telegram.

Although if he were honest with himself, he had to admit he was more than ready to return. He'd missed the place, missed the people. Missed Faith.

He'd hoped time and distance would cause her to fade from his memories, but she was as vibrant as ever, and not a night passed that he didn't dream about her.

Faith Leigh was the most beautiful woman he'd ever laid eyes on, although he hadn't always viewed her in that light. When she'd been born—wrinkled, red, and cater-wauling worse than any bawling calf he'd heard up until that moment—he'd proclaimed her to be butt-ugly. But she'd quickly managed to worm her way into his heart—not that he'd ever been too pleased about that.

He was probably somewhere between a decade and a dozen years older than she was. His true age was anyone's guess because the man who had called himself Rawley's pa hadn't paid much attention to the details of his life. It wasn't until Rawley went to live with Dallas and Cordelia Leigh that he learned people kept track of the time they spent on this earth. Since they'd taken him in on a cold night in December 1881, that had become the date when they honored his birth. He couldn't deny it was a good day for a little revelry because it marked the moment his life transformed from a mere existence into actually living.

As for Faith, her arrival had come in May 1884, duly noted and recorded in the family Bible. The last time he'd seen her had been six years earlier on the night she'd turned nineteen, after a celebration that had no doubt left a good many men—and possibly a few women—greeting the following morning with an aching head. He also suspected a number of cowboys had awakened a little heartsore because Faith had a way about her of making a man long for things he could never possess.

In the distance, the town came into view, and although it wasn't exactly as it had been when he left, he'd recognize it anywhere—the Grand Hotel dominating the skyline. It had been ahead of its time when it had been built in 1881. He'd seen much more of the country since then, but nothing else reminded him of a grand and majestic lady as much as it did, maybe because he'd long worshipped the woman who had envisioned and built it: Cordelia Leigh.

It was odd, all the emotions ricocheting through him. Pride, joy, a bit of remorse, a bit of dread. He had little doubt his abrupt departure had left many a burning question, and some might be wanting the answers with his return—but if he had his way, they'd go to the grave with him.

Faith Leigh stood on the depot platform and watched the smoke billowing from the behemoth in the distance bearing down on them. Her stomach knotted, and she took a deep breath to release the tension that had been building ever since she'd learned Rawley Cooper was on his way home.

She'd known this day would come, sooner or later. A reckoning. A chance to prove she was no longer the silly nineteen-year-old girl who had thrown herself at him and humiliated herself in the process.

The last time she'd seen him had been awkward at best. She expected it to be no different this time, especially when he learned all the truths about her—and he would. She'd never been able to hide anything from him. Once he'd been her best friend, her most trusted confidant, but then when she'd needed him the most, he'd ridden out of her life. Not that she blamed him, not deep down inside. But the girl she'd been still held a grudge.

She couldn't remember a time when she hadn't loved him. She hadn't learned to walk because her mother and father encouraged her; she'd taken those first steps because they'd provided the opportunity to keep up with Rawley. Not that her memories went back that far, but she knew herself well enough to know what had always motivated her, to know most of her actions had been an effort to tag along with the older boy her parents had taken in.

The train pulled into the station with a bellowing of steam and a screech of brakes. People disembarked in a frenzy as though anxious to get to where they were going or to greet the people they'd come to see.

All except him.

As though in no hurry, as though he had all day and the world would wait for him, Rawley Cooper stepped off the train, holding the saddle slung over his back with one hand at his shoulder. He was a tall drink of water who would quench any woman's thirst. Damn him. The past six years had served to make him more handsome, and a body that hard work on the range had honed to perfection had somehow managed to become even more pleasing to the eye.

He walked toward her with a lazy, loose-hipped stride that spoke of no rush to be anywhere, his boot heels thudding against the wooden platform, and she could feel it quivering with each step he took, just as she imagined women quivered whenever he gave them that sultry look through eyes so dark as to be almost black, as black as his hair. Just as she quivered now that he was near enough for her to see that he hadn't shaved recently. The short stubble added a ruggedness to his sharp jawline.

When he reached her, he used the thumb of his free hand to tip his black Stetson back from his brow, and the few shadows that had dared to play over his features retreated. At the corners of his eyes tiny lines fanned out, lines that hadn't been as deep before. A somberness hovered around him like a well-worn duster designed to protect against the harsh elements, and she wondered if he'd dreaded seeing her as much as she had him.

"Faith." No smile, no grin that had once brightened her world. Just the one word, spoken flatly, with no emotion, with no hint as to what he was feeling—and that in itself communicated everything.

She'd imagined this meeting a thousand times, hadn't slept a wink the night before, practicing just the right inflection, just the right words to greet him after all this time. They hovered on the tip of her tongue, but her fist beat them to the punch—literally—and she felt the jarring pain traveling up her arm before she'd even realized she'd given him a quick jab to the cheek, just below his eye, that had his head snapping back and his saddle hitting the wooden planks with a thud that caused them to shudder.

There was emotion now, rioting on his face, in his eyes. Fury. Shock. Disbelief. "What the hell, Faith?"

"That was for leaving without saying good-bye."

Chapter Two

Faith Leigh had a habit of speaking her mind and taking him by surprise. Based on the speed and force behind the punch, she'd been saving it up for six long years—suddenly all those months away seemed an eternity and seeing her again was a balm to his soul. His laughter was a bark, filled with pain and a bit of self-loathing. "I deserved that."

"I wouldn't have hit you if you didn't. Why'd you leave, Rawley?"

"You know why, Faith."

Her cheeks flamed red. "I was drunk."

Shaking his head, it took everything within him not to drop his gaze to the toes of his boots. "I wasn't."

Thank God for that, because otherwise a hell of a lot more friction would exist between them now.

"I hadn't expected anyone to be meeting me here," he added. Had he realized she'd greet him, he could have prepared himself a little more, although he'd known eventually they'd cross paths. He'd hoped for later, at the ranch, without witnesses and gawking strangers. For some reason, he'd expected tears, but the woman standing before him now wasn't the girl he'd walked out on.

She wore a dress of navy blue with a narrow skirt that didn't leave him guessing at the width of her hips. They'd broadened a bit during the intervening years, but then she had a little more meat on her everywhere. Suddenly the awkwardness was back because he shouldn't be noticing all that, shouldn't notice how maturity had added a grace to her features, or how grateful he was that the buttons went clear to her throat and that her puffed sleeves narrowed at her elbow and traveled down to her wrists, so he couldn't skim his gaze over her bared flesh. At a jaunty angle, she wore a small bonnet with light blue flowers, and he didn't want to think about removing it and unpinning her ebony hair to see if it was as long as it had been when he'd left.

"The buggy's over here," she said, as though acutely aware of the discomfort threatening to resettle between them.

"Let me get my horse. He's in the cattle car."

"Trust you to go to the trouble of bringing your horse when Uncle Houston could provide you with one easily enough."

Houston Leigh had made his living breeding, raising, and selling horses. Rawley figured few in the state didn't have at least one stallion, mare, or gelding that came from Leigh stock, including the one that was waiting for him. "Why leave good horseflesh behind?" Especially when he and the stallion were comfortable with each other, knew each other's quirks. He bent down to retrieve his saddle—

"Rawley Cooper!"

He barely had time to plant his feet and prepare himself before Maggie May Leigh had launched herself at him. He caught her and swung her around, relishing the tight band her arms made as they circled his neck, sent his hat flying. Houston's oldest daughter had taken after her mother, small and petite. If he hadn't known how stubborn and determined she could be, he might have feared he could break her, towering over her as he did.

"Put me down, you fool. I'm not a little girl anymore."

She certainly wasn't, but he'd known that before he left. He did as ordered, then reached down, snatched up his hat, and settled it back on his head, grateful some things never changed. Based on what he thought his age was, she was five years younger than he was, had clung to his shirttails until Faith had come along and become their little shadow.

"Brat," he groused, teasing her with the pet name he'd bestowed upon her when they were kids, gamely taking the smack to his shoulder she delivered before stepping back.

The hem of her slim black skirt dusted her ankles, and a neat black bow was knotted at the collar of her white shirt-waist. Atop her pinned-up blond hair sat a small, undecorated black hat, that of a woman with a mission. Her green eyes twinkled. "I was afraid I was going to miss you."

"How'd you even know I was coming in?" A stupid question in retrospect. The members of this family kept no secrets from one another, which was the reason he always held close his own.

"I'm a reporter. It's my business to know what's happening around here. The family is going to give you a chance to settle in tonight, then we'll all be over for dinner tomorrow."

"I'm looking forward to it." And he meant it. The Leigh clan was an immense, rowdy, rambunctious group of people who knew how to make a person feel right at home.

Reaching out, her brow furrowed, sadness mirrored in her eyes, she clutched his arm, her fingers creating shallow dents in his jacket. "I'm so sorry about Uncle Dallas."

His gut clenched as though she delivered the words along with a solid blow to his midsection. A cold shiver of dread skittered up his spine. He hadn't experienced this level of trepidation since he was a boy and had been unable to defend himself. "Dallas? What happened to Dallas?"

Her eyes widening with alarm, she looked at Faith. "Y'all didn't tell him?"

"Ma didn't want him worrying when it wouldn't change anything," Faith said, her face a mask of guilt.

"What the hell is going on, Faith?" he demanded, watching as emotions warred over her features—whether to be belligerent because of his tone or sympathetic to it—but he also spotted the worry, the concern, and maybe even a measure of fear. She crossed her arms over her chest as though needing to gird herself against whatever was going to roll off her tongue.

"Pa's been having some pains in his chest. You know they have to be bad for him to mention them to anyone. Doc thinks it's his heart. Pa thinks it's something he ate. But he passed out on the range a few days ago. Doc says he has to take it easy."

Which was the reason he'd been sent the telegram—because he was well and truly needed here. Suddenly he was hit with guilt for ever leaving in the first place. "I'll get my horse."

He said his good-byes to Maggie before reaching down to snag his saddle. With long strides that ate up the distance between him and the rear of the train, he approached the pinto that had already been unloaded for him. He'd always been partial to the spotted ponies ever since the Leigh brothers gave him one the first Christmas he spent with them more than a quarter of a century earlier. This latest, Shadow, he'd gotten from Houston shortly before he left. He flipped two bits to the station attendant before taking hold of the bridle. "Thanks, Charlie."

"Good to have you home, Rawley."

"Good to be home." A bit of a lie as he wished the circumstances were different.

He caught up with Faith, already sitting in the buggy tugging on her gloves, tossed his saddle and saddlebags in the compartment at the back, and secured Shadow there. The vehicle rocked as he climbed up onto the bench seat beside the girl who had constantly trailed after him when he was a boy. Without thinking, he reached for the reins, his hand brushing against hers as she did the same. They both froze. He hated their twin reactions because a time had existed when she'd nestled her hand snugly in his, when all he'd ever wanted was to protect her.

"I can drive," she said tartly.

"I know you can. I'm just being a gentleman."

She turned her head and held his gaze. "I've gotten used to doing for myself."

"You've always done for yourself, Faith. You're the most stubborn gal I ever met. You don't have to prove anything to me."

Fire darted out of those dark brown eyes and was quickly extinguished. She primly folded her hands in her lap. "Go on then."

He didn't argue further, didn't want to take time for it, but simply snatched up the reins, slapped them against the rumps of the two horses, and felt the tension ease a little as they got under way. "I'm anxious to get to the ranch. How bad is Dallas really?"

"Why won't you call him Pa?"

Because the man he'd known as Pa when he was a boy had been a mean, vindictive son of a bitch who had taken advantage of his mother, abducting her from the Shawnee people and getting a child on her that he hadn't wanted. Even after all these years, even knowing the man was dead, Rawley would still recoil and feel sick to his stomach when memories of him and that time in his life surfaced. Dallas might have raised him, but Dallas wasn't his pa. In Rawley's eyes he'd always been too big, too bold, as majestic as the land. Rawley had never felt worthy of acknowledging the man as his father. "He's not my pa," he said simply.

"But you call our mother Ma."

For the longest he'd simply known her as the pretty lady. When she'd opened her arms and heart to him, he'd gone to her with all that he was, desperate to fill the ache that lingered after his own mother—a kind, gentle soul who had loved him—died. "That's different."

"Care to explain how?"

"Not really. How bad off is Dallas?" he asked again.

She sighed heavily, obviously not pleased with his response or dogged determination to get back on topic, and he almost smiled because she'd always had far less patience with him than he'd had with her.

"Mostly he's just ornery because the doc doesn't want him doing anything strenuous. You know Pa. I don't think he's ever sat still for a moment in his life."

Except for the time when he'd almost died, but that was before Faith had come along.

"Is he sitting still?"

"Mostly he's wandering through the house, but at least he's not riding the range. He was by himself when he toppled from his horse. We don't know how long it was before someone ran across him."

Once more his gut tightened. He didn't want to think about Dallas passing over to the great beyond. As though sensing the direction of his thoughts, Faith patted his knee. "He claimed it was just the heat and maybe it was. To look at him, you wouldn't know anything had happened."

But something *had* happened, and Rawley hadn't been there—because of the woman sitting beside him, someone for whom inappropriate thoughts and feelings had blossomed, and he hadn't been sure he could keep them in check. When she'd challenged him one night, he'd realized his restraint was thinly tethered and could easily snap. Where would they be then?

He'd grown up in the bosom of her family, knew himself not to be worthy of her. So he'd left. To protect her, to protect himself. Yet he couldn't tell her all that. Instead, he settled into mentally berating and beating himself up for making himself even more unworthy by not staying and being the man he needed to be, the man Dallas Leigh had raised him to be.

Glancing over at her, he was struck by how much he'd missed her, how very little he knew about what had transpired with her since he'd left. It seemed no matter how far or fast he traveled, she was always there. During the years he'd been gone, he'd only ever written letters to Ma, received news from her. Whenever he arrived at the next town, he'd send her a telegram to let her know he was doing all right and a postcard to give her a sense of his surroundings. It became easier three years ago, when Congress authorized using half of the back of the postcard for scrawling notes. He no longer had to sit down and write out a lengthy letter to her. A few lines, short and sweet, was all he needed to keep her apprised of his situation.

"What are you doing these days, Faith? Your oil wells come in?" After Spindletop, she'd been optimistic they might find oil on some of the Leigh spread and had begun working with oilmen who had the skills to help her locate it.

"They never amounted to much," she said. "I lost interest in them. These days I'm mostly just looking after the ranch."

He wasn't surprised she was in charge of the spread. She was the logical choice, would inherit all of it someday. "How's that going?"

She latched on to the opportunity to talk about something other than themselves, to wax on about the cattle, the goings-on with the men, the ones who had passed, the ones who had retired. Listening with interest, absorbing the sound of her voice, warmed him in ways nothing else did.

The road from town hadn't changed much. Barbed wire lined both sides of it, wire he'd restrung and repaired countless times, wire that had changed the cattle industry. The days of the long cattle drives were behind them. They just had to get the cattle to a train. He wondered if a time would come when there wouldn't be any cowboys at all. Sometimes he felt like a dying breed.

He turned the horses from the road onto a narrower path that passed beneath an archway bearing the two D's that marked the brand Dallas had begun using when he'd married Cordelia McQueen, known as Dee among her family and friends. Not that Rawley had ever called her that. From the moment she'd made him hers, she'd been Ma.

Eventually the house came into view. "Just as hideous as I remember," he said with fondness. It was a monstrosity, had the look of a castle on the prairie. Dallas had built the massive structure more than thirty years earlier in anticipation of the arrival of his mail-order bride. Only destiny had found Amelia Carson falling in love with Houston Leigh when he'd been sent to Fort Worth to fetch her on Dallas's behalf.

"When I was younger, I always felt like a princess living there," Faith said quietly.

"Dallas sure spoiled you like you were one."

"You did your fair share of spoiling. It's a wonder I learned to walk the way you carried me everywhere."

Surprised, he glanced over at her. "You remember that?"

She shook her head. "No, but Ma told me often enough. 'That Rawley Cooper would never let you out of his sight.' Apparently I ensured it by constantly holding my arms up to you."

Her voice held teasing, but his watching out for her had been a serious thing. He'd been responsible for Cordelia Leigh losing her first baby—no matter that everyone said it wasn't his fault. He knew the truth of it and had been determined that nothing was going to happen to take her beloved daughter from her.

As they neared the house, he could see the outbuildings, all the activity going on. Work on the Leigh spread never seemed to slow or stop. He imagined he'd be able to pick up the rhythm as though he'd never been away.

Then he spotted Dallas and Ma sitting on the front porch on the bench swing, moving slowly, lazily, an unfamiliar scruffy hound resting nearby. He barely had time to realize that a coverall-clad little girl in boots was sitting between them before Ma had shoved herself to her feet. He brought the buggy to a halt—

Everything seemed to happen at a speed that made it impossible to comprehend.

The child was rushing down the steps. "Mama!"

Racing after her, the dog bounded off the porch.

Faith quickly clambered out of the buggy, dashed forward, snatched the girl up before she got too close to the horses, and swung her around, their laughter echoing joyously on the air.

Setting the brake, Rawley climbed off the bench, his feet hitting the ground with a thud, stirring up the dust, his body no longer seeming connected to his brain, moving independently of any thoughts he might have.

Suddenly arms were around his back, squeezing tightly, holding him close. His ma. His ma was there, welcoming him home. Damn, but he'd missed her, which he figured was probably obvious to her since his hug was a little too strong. He'd always loved the fragrance of her, the warmth of her. She was all that was good and clean in his life.

Wrapping her hands around his upper arms, she leaned back and smiled at him. Her face contained a few more wrinkles, her dark hair a few more strands of gray, but damn if she wasn't a sight for sore eyes. "You're looking good," she said, so much tenderness woven into her voice that if he wasn't a grown man, he might have wept.

When she released her hold on him and stepped back, Dallas moved in, his dark hair and mustache sprinkled with white, but he still looked capable of commanding the world as he pumped Rawley's hand, slapped his shoulder. "Welcome home, son."

Son. Dallas had called him that through the years more times than he could count, his throat always tightening as the truth bombarded him: He wasn't the man's son. Dallas's son was lying in a grave beneath a nearby windmill because of

Rawley's cowardice. Still, he responded with a brusque nod, grateful Dallas appeared more robust than he'd expected.

A corner of Dallas's mouth shifted up. "Faith give you that bruise coming up on your cheek?"

He'd hoped her punch hadn't left a mark, but considering how tender his cheek felt, he figured it would look worse tomorrow. "Seems she took exception to the way I left."

"She did indeed."

"She told me about your ticker but, Dallas, you're not that old."

Dallas laughed. "Son, I'm the oldest man I know."

He was sixty-three, which was fairly ancient for the life he'd lived, but Rawley couldn't help but believe—hope—he had a few more years left in him.

Rawley might have offered more words but he was distracted, his attention focused on Faith and the imp perched on her hip who reminded him of Faith when she'd been about that size. The child was talking nonstop, words he couldn't hear, but Faith merely nodded and smiled, her eyes occasionally widening as though she were impressed.

Faith must have felt his gaze boring into her, because she finally looked over at him, and a deep scarlet blush crept up her face, peaked at her cheeks. Her smile withering as she began sauntering over alerted him that he hadn't seen a true grin from her since he'd arrived, not that he'd really expected one. The last time they were together he could have handled things better. He realized that now.

The dog sniffing his legs grew bored and wandered off. Her parents parted like they were the Red Sea and she was

Moses. She angled up that pert little chin of hers. Her brown eyes held a challenge and a threat—as though she feared he might do something to cause harm to the child she held, the one who had called her Mama. When the hell had she gotten married, and why the hell hadn't anyone told him?

"Callie, this is your uncle Rawley."

Even knowing what the introduction would entail hadn't prepared him for the way the words battered him—a series of uppercuts to his heart. Then the sprite smiled at him and his chest threatened to implode, the tightness of it making it nearly impossible to draw in a breath. She was her mother all over again, sweet, innocent, pure. Waving her fingers at him, she nestled her head against Faith's shoulder.

"This is my daughter."

"I gathered as much." He hadn't meant for the words to come out so terse, but a thousand questions bombarded him. "Congratulations. I didn't realize you'd gotten married."

"I didn't."

CHAPTER THREE

She should have told him, should have prepared him. She deserved her mother's disapproving, narrow-eyed stare because Ma had insisted Faith needed to tell Rawley about Callie before they got to the ranch, but the right moment to do so never arrived—or maybe she hadn't been looking for it. "I gave birth to a child out of wedlock" wasn't something that easily slipped itself into conversation. Or perhaps she'd simply feared his censure, his judgment. There had been a time when his opinion had mattered more than breathing.

Suddenly he clapped his large hands together, making her jump, and spread them out toward Callie. "Want to come to your uncle Rawley?"

His voice held such tenderness, such devotion that he was once again the person she'd always adored. All the anger and resentment she'd been hoarding since his departure shrank somewhat, making her realize how silly she'd been to think that he, of all people, would sit in judgment of her. It had never been his way. When she'd been jealous of some of the other girls and tried to enlist him in making fun of them—even when only in the quietness of sitting beneath the stars with no one around to hear—he'd refused to cooperate, to say anything unkind about anyone. "I ain't walking in their shoes."

Callie, who had yet to meet a stranger, was halfway out of Faith's arms and into Rawley's before Faith could react, suspended between the two of them, joining them, re-establishing a bond she'd feared had snapped with his leaving. With a self-conscious chortle, she quickly released her daughter's legs, confident he had a firm grip on the precious child, wouldn't let her fall. She didn't want to consider how right it looked for Callie to be balanced on his lean hip, one of her thin arms slung around his neck, her brown eyes sparkling with glee, and her smile large enough to reveal nearly every tooth, including the gap where she'd recently lost her first one.

"How old are you?" Rawley asked.

"Five." With her fingers and thumb splayed out, she fairly pressed her palm to his nose, so he could easily count the years.

"Well, you're a big girl, aren't you?"

"Uh-huh." She bobbed her head with enough force that her brown braids bounced against her shoulders. "How old are you?"

"Don't rightly know for sure. Somewhere north of thirty, I reckon."

She laughed, the sweet, innocent tinkling of a child who had never known hurt. "You're funny."

With a grin, he reached into his pocket and pulled out a sarsaparilla stick. "Want some?"

Callie nodded enthusiastically. Even while holding her daughter, he managed to snap it in two and hand her a piece. Faith's heart tightened so painfully with the memories of all the times he'd shared his candy with her that she was afraid tears were going to flood her eyes.

"Rawley Cooper, you know better than to go about spoiling your supper," Ma chided, the affection in her voice belying any scolding she may have meant to give.

"I'll still be hungry enough to eat a horse. What about you, Callie?"

She shook her head, taking the stick out of her mouth. "We don't eat horses. We eat cows. 'N chickens, 'n pigs, 'n rabbits."

"Do you now?" he asked, as though truly interested in her eating habits.

She nodded. "Grampa once ate a snake." She scrunched up her face. "Yuck. I don't like snakes."

"Me either."

"Well, no one will be eating snakes tonight," Ma said. "Come on. I'm sure the cook has dinner waiting on us by now."

"I need to see to the buggy and horses," Rawley said.

"Pete's handling that chore," Pa told him before raising his arm toward the ranch hand who had already taken hold of the lead horse and was starting to move everything toward the barn.

Rawley turned, the smile he bestowed on the aging man genuine, and Faith wished he'd greeted her with the same glad-to-see-you grin. "Hey, Pete."

"Hey, Rawley. Glad to have you back."

"Glad to be back."

Although Faith heard the truth in his tone, she couldn't help but believe he might be feeling a bit disoriented discovering how very little remained the same since he'd left.

Ma slipped her arm around his waist. "You've gotten skinny."

Not that skinny, Faith thought. She could see evidence of his muscles filling out the sleeve of his jacket as he held her daughter.

"You probably want to wash up after your trip," her mother continued. "Your old room upstairs is all ready for you."

A flicker of surprise crossed his face, no doubt because he'd moved out of the residence years before he left.

"Callie and I are living in your cabin," Faith said quickly, drawing his attention. With her, he shuttered his emotions, so she couldn't tell what he was thinking—and that unsettled her. "If you're staying we can pack up and come back to the house."

"No, that's fine. Stay where you are."

She wondered if his answer meant he was only going to be here temporarily. Fearing he might question her regarding the details of her life if she questioned him, she hadn't bothered to ask him what he'd been up to since he left. She knew he'd been herding cattle, but maybe he'd also met someone. However, if he had, wouldn't he have brought her with him? "I'll take Callie. She's all sticky now. Her face and hands could use a good scrubbing."

"Nooo!" her daughter cried, burying her face in the curve of his neck. "Save me, Uncle Rawley."

As though she'd kicked him in the heart and was truly in some sort of danger, he appeared stunned, a little shaken, uncertain as to how to handle the situation in order to best protect her.

"Don't be such a silly goose," Faith said, working her arms around her daughter until they were forming a barrier between her and Rawley, until she could feel the firmness of his chest. Not skinny at all. She wanted to jerk back. Instead she pried Callie free.

"I'll take her," Ma said with an authority that had Callie going to her without any fuss at all.

Faith watched as her mother and father began wandering toward the house, as Rawley sauntered to the end of the porch where Pete had left his saddlebags. Reluctantly, she followed him over, knowing she had things she needed to say, if she could only find the right words. But she'd been searching for them ever since she found out he was returning, and they still eluded her.

"Who's her father?" he asked flatly, reaching down, grabbing the bags, and slinging them over a shoulder before turning to face her.

"Just a cowboy with no plans to stay."

"He left you?" Anger slithered through his voice. Had he

been here when she realized she was with child, he'd have probably tracked the poor fellow down.

"We weren't—" She shook her head, planted her hands on her hips, and kicked the toe of her shoe into the ground. Finally, she lifted her gaze and met his. "It's complicated."

"No, it's not, Faith. He was with you, he got you pregnant, and he just skipped on out of your life? That's not how it works."

"I didn't want to marry him."

"Why the hell not?"

"Because he didn't measure up." *Because he wasn't you.*

As though her answer explained everything, she spun on her heel and headed into the house, leaving Rawley with the certainty there was more to the story than Faith was letting on. Once she'd confided everything to him, but his departure had created distance between them—which had been his intention, only he'd expected to limit it to miles traveled, not trust wavering. So much needed to be said, so many amends made, but not now with dusk on the horizon and people waiting on them.

Traveling a path he'd journeyed hundreds of times, he stepped onto the porch and wandered into the house, where the fragrance of home wafted around him. No other place he'd ever visited smelled like this, like warmth, welcome, and love. The entryway was cavernous, but the rugs stifled the echo of his footsteps as he made his way to the stairs. He remembered the first time he'd ascended them, the fear and shame that had accompanied him. Now he trudged up with the confidence of a man who knew himself, knew his place in the world was wherever he wanted it to be.

At the landing he turned down the hallway and walked to the last room on the left. The first night he'd stayed there, Dallas had given him a key so he could lock himself in, lock other people out. Later, lying in that bed, staring at the ceiling, he'd felt safe, an unfamiliar peace coming over him. He'd thought he'd never want to leave.

It was a belief that stayed with him until the night Faith had come to his cabin—

Shoving back those memories, he pushed open the door and strode into the room where he'd sleep until it was once again time to make himself scarce.

Chapter Four

"I have a horse and a calf and a dog"—the scruffy mutt was sitting quietly frozen and at attention beside her chair—"and a chicken. I want a el'phant. Do you know what a el'phant is?"

"I do," Rawley said from his place across the table from the little minx, who hadn't stopped talking since they'd all taken a seat. "I've even seen one."

"Me too!"

"A circus came through last summer," Faith explained before he could ask where she'd seen one. It might have been the same traveling menagerie show he'd visited during his short stint in Colorado.

"I like el'phants," Callie stated emphatically, looking longingly at her mother.

"We're not getting one," Faith said patiently.

The child turned her earnest attention back to him. "Do you like el'phants?"

"I like looking at them. I wouldn't want to have one about, though. It makes a lot of mess. You'd have to spend your day shoveling out its stalls, then washing and feeding it. You wouldn't have any time for playing."

Her tiny brow furrowed as though she was seriously weighing the effort to have an elephant against her other choices. "I can swim. Can you?"

He reckoned with that blurted question, the topic was moving on from animals. "I can."

"I swim in the river but only if someone is watching. Want to swim with me?"

"Maybe."

"When?"

"Callie, do you remember the rule about talking at the table?" Dallas asked.

The little sprite twisted her mouth and gave him a sly look out of the corner of her eye, as though not facing him directly would prevent him from seeing her displeasure at the question. "I'm to be seen, not heard."

Dallas gave a brusque nod. "That's right."

Callie gave an identical brusque nod, before quietly picking up a pea between her tiny forefinger and thumb and offering it to the dog.

Rawley glanced over at Faith, who was struggling not to smile, and for a moment they were both kids at the very same table, determined to obey Dallas's edict—children did not talk unless spoken to. The first time Dallas had asked Rawley his opinion during a meal, he'd been so taken off guard as to jerk forcefully enough to nearly topple over his chair. Only later did he realize Dallas was acknowledging he was grown.

It was a wonder he'd survived Faith's glare because she'd obviously not liked one bit that he had come into possession of a privilege denied to her.

He turned his attention back to the child who was quickly snagging his heart. She delicately picked up another pea and offered it to the dog, who gladly took it. Then she squarely met Rawley's gaze and leaned toward him slightly.

"I don't like peas," she said in what he could only assume she thought was a whisper, but her voice carried over the table. "But Rufus does. Do you like peas?"

"I do, and do you know why?"

Her eyes widened—either because he'd surprised her by answering instead of scolding her for breaking the rule or because she was truly interested—and she shook her head, stretching farther over her plate as though he was about to impart some wondrous secret.

"They make you grow tall and run fast."

"I can run fast already."

"Bet you can't beat me."

She narrowed her eyes, bit her bottom lip in concentration, as though striving to determine if she should challenge him. "Can you run faster than Mama?"

He still wasn't accustomed to Faith being a mother, to her daughter referring to her as such. A part of him continued to see Faith as a young girl, while another part had to admit she was anything but—especially when her eyes held a challenge, daring him to suppose for even a minute he could outrace her. He wondered about the man who had caught her, made her his own, and then abandoned her. He wasn't happy about her keeping secrets from him. "Absolutely."

Faith scoffed. "I'd like to see you try, Rawley Cooper."

The words were tossed out easily, as though no years had passed, as though no distance had come between them. "You were fast, Faith, but I was always faster. You know that."

"But you haven't spent five years running after this little one." She tilted her head toward her daughter.

He was slammed with regret, regret that he hadn't been here for her. If he'd known, he'd have returned straightaway. He'd have made the damn fool who got her with child marry her. He wondered why the hell Dallas hadn't.

It was the longest meal of her life. Maybe because her stomach was knotted up so tightly she could barely eat, or maybe because she didn't know what Callie might blurt, or maybe, just maybe, it was because the sight of Rawley caused emotions to keep welling up. With his leaving, he'd made his position regarding her clear. But a part of her still longed for his arms to circle around her.

"All right, Little Bit, time for us to go. Give everyone a hug," she announced. She watched as her parents embraced her child, her heart squeezing as it always did because they so accepted her daughter. She knew not all parents would.

She didn't think it was possible for her chest to tighten any further until Callie rushed with open arms toward Rawley. Her screech echoed around them as he swung her up and over his shoulder, wrapped her arms about his neck before placing his below her butt, giving her a sturdy perch to rest on as her legs curled around his sides, her feet dangling just shy of his chest. "I'll escort you home."

She didn't much like the way her nerve endings came to attention as though he'd offered a far more intimate service. "That's not necessary. It's not that far. We'll be fine."

"It's getting dark."

Laughing lightly, she hated the thread of panic roughening the sound. "We've traveled this path a thousand times."

"Still."

The single word held determination and reflected the obstinacy of a man who had made up his mind. She almost punched him. He'd used that tone on her countless times when she was a girl, but now she was a woman—

Only he didn't wait for her to rebuff him. He simply headed for the door, her daughter bouncing excitedly against his back. "Won't be long," he called over his shoulder to her parents.

Her mother arched a brow at her, challenging her to make things right between herself and Rawley. Faith gave her a quick hug, then one to her father. "See you tomorrow."

She raced out after Rawley, striving not to accept how natural it seemed, not to recall how many times she'd done so as a child, always chasing after him, always wanting to be in the middle of whatever he was doing. When she caught up to him, she was grateful her long strides matched his. She'd always wanted to be his equal.

Together they saddled the horses in silence. She didn't

particularly like the way her heart gave a little tug when he lifted Callie onto her pony.

They were well past the house, Rufus running in circles around them, Callie laughing before Rawley said quietly, "Dallas looks good," and she realized he hadn't insisted on escorting her home because he'd thought she couldn't take care of herself, but because he'd needed to talk, had needed her.

"I know. He doesn't appear to be a man suffering from any ailments. Maybe it *was* something he ate, maybe it *was* the heat, but it sure gave us all a fright."

"I noticed you hugged them both pretty tightly."

The sun was just an orange line on the horizon. "I've come to realize they're getting older, and I could lose one or both of them at any time. They are so much a part of this place, a part of my life, I can't imagine not having them around."

"It'll be a while yet." He said it with such confidence that she had no choice except to believe—or at least want to believe—him.

"We're home!" Callie yelled, as though they couldn't see the small cabin nestled among the mesquite trees.

When they brought the horses to a halt, he dismounted, grabbed Callie, and swung her to the ground. As soon as her feet hit the dirt, she was off chasing fireflies, Rufus leaping along beside her.

"You used to do that," Rawley said fondly.

"Remember when you caught some and put them in a jar for me, so I could sleep with them beside my bed?" He'd always done little things like that for her. Small wonder she'd loved him so much, still did.

"I remember. Before you went to sleep you set them free."

She stared at him in disbelief. Not wanting to hurt his feelings, she'd been incredibly quiet creeping to her window, opening the jar, and sending the bugs back into the night. "You knew about that?"

"Faith, there wasn't much you did that I didn't know about." He nodded toward Callie. "Didn't know about her, though. Why didn't you tell me about her?"

"Why did you really leave?" she fired back at him.

His answer was a half grin. "It's complicated."

Her own words tossed back at her should have angered her, but only served to sadden her. "We never used to keep secrets from each other."

His smile turned somber, his eyes filled with regret. "We always had secrets. Or at least I did. I'll see to your horses."

"I'll help."

They worked in silence, relaxing into old, familiar routines. When the horses were settled in the corral with its protective shelter, Faith headed up the steps to the front porch. "Thanks for escorting us home."

He stood with his hands pressed into the back pockets of his denim pants, a familiar stance that tugged at her heart. He studied her as though he had more to say and didn't know quite how to say it. He wasn't alone in that regard. Maybe she owed him an apology. Her recollection of that night was blurred, faint, but she couldn't seem to find the words, not when so much between them had changed.

Callie bounded up the steps and hugged one of the porch

beams that supported the eaves like it was her best friend. "Grampa helped me teach Rufus to play dead. Wanna see?"

"Sure," Rawley said, and Faith had a feeling he wouldn't deny her anything she asked.

She pointed her tiny finger at the dog. "Rufus, drop dead!"

The dog fell to his side.

"That's pretty impressive," Rawley said, looking over at Faith. "I can't believe Dallas had the patience to train the mutt to do that."

"He always had a way of making people obey. I guess that talent transfers to animals, too. He'll stay like that . . . Callie, let him know the game's over."

"Rufus, wake up!"

The dog jumped up and raced off, no doubt catching sight of something in need of chasing.

"Uncle Rawley, wanna see my pichers?" Callie asked, and Faith knew the child could spend all night sharing one thing after another.

"I'm sure Uncle Rawley is tired," Faith told her. "We need to let him get back to Gramma's."

"Actually I'm not," he said. Reaching out, he tweaked Callie's nose, making her giggle. "I'd like to see your pictures."

"It's time for her to go to bed," Faith said patiently.

"How long can it take?" he asked.

"Please, Mama," Callie pleaded, clasping her tiny hands together and holding them as though in prayer. "Please."

Damn it. She'd yet to learn how to deny her child anything. But she didn't want Rawley coming inside her cabin, what had once been his cabin. She didn't want to remember the last time she'd been with him—inside those walls.

Did those memories mean nothing to him? Maybe if they were rekindled she'd find out the true reason for his leaving.

"I guess a few more minutes won't hurt. Come on in."

He didn't know why he'd pushed it. The last thing he wanted was to dredge up memories of the last time he'd been with Faith, but it was hard to let go of the habit of wanting time with her.

Stepping over the threshold, he inhaled the fragrance of wildflowers, a mixture of scents, no bloom in particular standing out. It was the scent of Faith. She'd always smelled of things wild and untamed. Against his will, his gaze jumped to the doorway that led into the bedroom. He could see the same quilt draped over the bed, fought against remembering how peaceful and right Faith had looked stretched out over it when he'd leaned against the doorjamb and absorbed the sight of her, every inch from her bare feet to her messed hair, before he'd strode out of the cabin for the last time.

He jerked his attention away from places it shouldn't roam and took in the remainder of the cabin. Another door, one that hadn't been there before, indicated they'd added a room. No doubt for Callie. The furniture in the main room remained the same, but a rocker had been added, and his chest tightened with the image of Faith rocking her daughter. She'd added frilly yellow curtains to the windows and

paintings of cowboys rustling steers to the walls. That was
Faith: a combination of femininity and masculinity. She'd
never shied away from the tough jobs.

"Uncle Rawley, sit here."

Glancing over, he watched as Callie patted the cushion
beside her on the sofa. A small book rested in her lap. Damn,
if she didn't have the biggest, brownest eyes he'd ever seen.
He looked over at Faith, knowing she wanted to be rid of
him, that he was making a nuisance of himself.

She gave a quick bob of her head as she settled into the
rocker. "Go on."

Dropping on to the sofa, he laid his arm along its back.
Even sitting, he towered over the little girl. She gingerly
folded back the leather cover as though it was deserving of
her reverence, and his breath caught as she placed her index
finger in the middle of a postcard.

"That's the Grand Canyon," she announced with authority. "I'm gonna go see it someday."

He'd sent the postcard to Ma to relieve her worries and
so she could appreciate one of the wonders he was seeing, had
expected she'd share the postcards with others, but hadn't
considered that they'd be kept.

Another page turned, another postcard. "A hotel in Santa
Fe," she said as though she knew where Santa Fe was. "I'm
gonna go there."

Another page turned, another postcard. "A dining room
in Ar'zona. Goin' there, too."

A dining room in a Fred Harvey hotel. Many of the postcards came from the hotels where he stayed for a night. He

had sent them in particular so his ma could see that all the lodgings paled in comparison to the Grand Hotel she'd built in Leighton. He lifted his gaze to Faith. "You kept them?"

"I was fascinated by them," she admitted. "I imagined you walking those streets, eating at those tables, sleeping in those beds."

"More often than not, I slept beneath the stars."

"I imagined that, too. I figured a lot of those were sent to make Ma believe you were living better than you were."

"A train station in Cal'forn'a," Callie announced as though his attention hadn't detoured away from her. "We have trains here. I'm gonna ride it when I'm bigger."

"Are you?" he asked.

She bobbed her head, even as she turned another page. "They're faster 'n horses."

"But they're not very good company," he said.

She twisted around to look up at him, a question in those brown eyes that were so much like her mother's.

"I talk to my horse all the time," he told her.

"'Bout what?"

"My dreams." He leaned in and whispered, "I can tell it my secrets. It won't tell anyone."

"I won't tell, either."

"Promise?"

She nodded with such enthusiasm her braids were flapping around her.

"Your ma was right. I'm tired. It's been a long day. But I'll come back and look at the rest another time. How about that?"

"'Kay."

Displaying the same reverence with which she'd opened the book, she closed it. He pushed himself to his feet while Faith simultaneously rose from the rocker, and they both stood there awkwardly, he with his hands shoved in the pockets at the back of his pants, she with her hands clasped in front of her.

"Thanks for indulging her," Faith finally said.

"She's quite the pistol."

Faith smiled, the first genuine one she'd given to him since meeting him at the depot, and it caused a pain in his chest that made him wonder if he was suffering from the same affliction as Dallas. "She is that. If you're not careful, she'll wrap you around her littlest finger."

"That warning comes a little too late." He glanced around. "I'm surprised you'd want to live here."

"It wasn't being used. You said you were tired, so we shouldn't keep you." She hurried to the door, as though a coyote was nipping at her heels, and opened it. "We'll see you tomorrow—at the gathering if nowhere else."

The gathering, when the remainder of the family would descend on him like locusts, wanting answers. Reaching back with a wink, he tugged on one of Callie's braids. "Sweet dreams."

She gave him such an innocent smile that he wanted her to never have anything but the most pleasant of images racing through her head. The things in his tended to be ugly, made for a lot of restless nights. When he got to the threshold, he stopped beside Faith. She no longer wore braids, leaving him nothing to tug. He remembered a time when he might have leaned over to buss a kiss over her cheek. But those days were long behind them. "Night, Faith."

She merely nodded, closing the door on him as soon as his boot heels were clear of it.

Taking a meandering path back to the house, he passed a cow or two along the way, feeling small and insignificant with the vast sky above him. Darkness settled in, bringing with it black velvet dotted with stars and a sliver of a moon. One of the reasons he enjoyed working with cattle was because he never felt hemmed in, because the horizon was always in the distance, beckoning, promising more space beyond it. It had once satisfied, but now it suddenly seemed empty. And he felt that a chunk of his life had been lived without him really being a part of it. What an odd thought to be nagging at him as he climbed the steps and went into the house.

A lamp had been left burning on a table in the entryway, so he suspected Dallas and Ma had already retired. He was surprised Dallas hadn't gone to the trouble of having electricity introduced out here but figured it would come in time. Picking up the lamp, he made his way to the large library where he'd learned to love books, set the lamp on the marble-topped table that held an assortment of crystal decanters, poured a generous amount of whiskey into a tumbler, and stepped through a door onto the veranda. Leaning against a beam, he took a slow sip and looked out on the familiar, the land stretching before him for miles, the occasional shadowy windmill standing proud. He'd built a couple in his day, had always enjoyed the strenuous labor of it.

A gentle hand landed between his shoulder blades, rubbed the tightness there, skimmed over his shoulders before drifting away. Turning his head slightly, he looked over at the second woman he had ever loved, the first being his mother—or at least his memory of her, faded and frayed as it was. "Why didn't you tell me Faith had a daughter?"

"She asked us not to. Whatever your reasons for leaving, she didn't want to be the reason you came back."

He'd have married her without hesitation to spare her the shame and embarrassment of being an unwed mother. "Do you know who the father is?"

Turning, she pressed her back against the beam and met his gaze head-on. "If you want answers, you'll have to talk to Faith. She's the one who decides what people know when it comes to Callie."

"She's being tight-lipped."

"That's her prerogative. I suspect there are things you never shared with her." Slipping in against his side, she wrapped her arms around him. "I'm glad you're home."

In one smooth movement, he set his glass on the railing and enfolded her in his embrace, holding her securely. "You know Dallas is too ornery to die."

She laughed lightly, but he heard the whisper of encroaching tears, the edge of worry. "I know. Still, everything needs to be set right between you and Faith."

After his mother gave him another hug and went back inside, he lowered himself to the top step, stretched out his legs, and breathed in the warm Texas air, traveling back in his memories to the night everything changed.

Chapter Five

May 1903

With a great deal of amusement, Rawley sat astride his horse, watching as Faith bossed the oilmen around. While Leigh money and land was making the search for the inky black pools possible, Faith had her opinions on the matter and a way about her of making folks listen. She took after her father in that regard.

Rawley didn't know if in the middle of the jaw wagging someone said something to her regarding his presence or if she just sensed it, but suddenly she swung around, smiled broadly, and waved. "Rawley!"

Her strides ate up the ground separating them. Like her mother, she was tall, only an inch or two shorter than him. A man didn't have to wonder about the length of her legs because when she was out on the range, she wore denim pants that outlined that sweet little backside—

He shoved that inappropriate thought into a dark corner. More and more lately, he was beginning to view her as a woman in her own right, and those thoughts were entirely wrong coming from him. He shouldn't be thinking about the way her white shirt tucked into her pants at her narrow waist, leaving very little regarding her shape to a man's imagination. The long braid of her ebony hair was draped over her shoulder, flapped against her chest with the quickness of her steps. He remembered her lamenting the absence of a bosom when she was about fourteen. She certainly had no reason to complain about that now since her chest was far removed from resembling a plank of wood. She was all curves.

To avoid her throwing her arms around him like she usually did when they crossed paths—a habit from her growing-up days when he'd cart her around because she was too small to keep up—he stayed in the saddle and waited.

When she reached him, she laid the flat of her bare hand on his thigh. Even knowing it was an innocent gesture didn't stop the shock of pleasure from traveling through him, not that he gave any indication he held anything other than companionable feelings for her.

"Are you pondering the notion of coming over to our side?" she asked, grinning up at him, her brown eyes teasing with mischievousness.

"Hell no. I can't believe Dallas is letting you poke holes in his land."

"You'll feel differently when they discover oil." She dug her fingers into his thigh. "They'll be drilling by the end of the month."

"It's a fool's errand, Faith."

"They found that gusher in Spindletop."

Pockets of oil had long pooled on the surface in some areas of Texas, but two years earlier when that gusher hit, oilmen started taking a real interest in what the state might have to offer below the ground.

"That's miles away, on the other side of the state. Out here it's only land, cattle, and windmills."

"You never did have much imagination." With a sigh, she crossed her arms below her breasts, twisted about, and leaned against his leg. "There's oil out there. I feel it deep in my bones."

"Then I hope you find it."

Tilting up her face, she looked at him. "The cattle industry is changing. You're the last of a breed, Rawley. Cowboys aren't going to be riding the range for much longer. You don't even have long cattle drives any more. You just herd those little dogies to the train depot."

Where they were simply led onto the cattle cars and carted to the slaughterhouse. It was a little too sterile for him, but it was also a lot less work and required fewer nights trekking across dangerous terrain. "Still plenty of work to be done. Like fencing off these few acres of land so the cattle aren't bothering your drillers."

The bright smile she bestowed upon him always caused the dark storms threatening his soul to retreat for a while. "And I appreciate that."

Fighting back the urge to lean down and capture her mouth, he merely brought the brim of his hat lower, hoping the shadows would camouflage the yearnings that sometimes overtook him when it came to her. He'd spent a good bit of his life knowing she was destined to break his heart. Reaching into his shirt pocket, he pulled out a sarsaparilla stick.

"Gimme," she said, holding up her hand.

"It's my last one."

"It's always your last one."

Breaking it in half, he handed her a piece, just as he had for most of her life.

Shifting his gaze, he watched as the leader of this drilling outfit began sauntering toward them. Cole Berringer. Rawley knew his dislike for the oilman stemmed from the fact he was spending his days in Faith's company, and she'd taken a fancy to him. Berringer had approached Dallas a few months ago with his belief that oil was to be found on Leigh land. While Dallas hadn't been that interested, Faith had embraced the prospect of possibilities. Normally, Rawley supported Faith's enthusiasm for trying out new things and would have encouraged her in this endeavor if Berringer wasn't such a handsome devil, with his wheat-colored hair and blue eyes. He had half the ladies in town swooning over him.

"Cooper," the man said, stopping a few feet away. His brown pants and jacket showed little wear, the sign of a man who preferred giving orders to doing the hard work.

"Berringer."

"Don't see a lot of men who still go around with a six-gun strapped to their thigh."

Rawley shrugged, not feeling the need to defend himself but determined to follow the code of politeness under which he'd been raised. "I do a lot of solitary riding. It brings me a measure of peace."

"It's not as though there are any outlaws or renegades lurking about."

"We've had a few head go missing the past month or so. I'd say we still have thieves."

"But the state is civilized now. You let the law—"

Rawley caught a movement—

Had his gun drawn, palmed, and fired before his next blink. And took great satisfaction in Berringer squealing like a pig whose tail had been yanked. He was crouched down, his hands over his head in a protective gesture.

"What the hell, Cooper?"

Having been trained by Houston, who sold horses to the military, not to bolt at a gun's report, Rawley's stallion had done little more than give a slight sidestep. All the men had stilled. Faith merely stared at him questioningly, waiting to determine if he was in need of a scolding for terrifying a man she obviously thought well of. Rawley pointed the barrel off to the side a bit, before sliding the six-shooter back into the leather. "Rattler."

In horror, Berringer stared at the mutilated reptile, then glared at Rawley. "I didn't hear it rattling. You could have given some warning."

"They don't always buzz before they strike. I've run across enough of them that struck without making a sound not to take a chance on its mood. Besides, it was coiled and lunging your way by the time I saw it."

"That's true, boss," a fellow with a shovel said as he approached. "I was trying to get over here to kill it without making any noise. Didn't want to alarm it, cause it to attack— but then it shot toward you . . . I'd say it meant business."

"Fine, Jones," Berringer said impatiently. "Get back to work." He removed his hat, slapped it against his leg, stirring up a cloud of dust.

Rawley took no pleasure from seeing the man's hand trembling. Or at least he fought not to. He did experience a bit of satisfaction in unsettling Berringer. He was going to burn in hell for his unkind thoughts, but then he was headed there even with kind thoughts, so what did it matter?

"Reckon I owe you," Berringer said grudgingly.

"Just making sure cowboys stay relevant."

The man's jaw tightened. "Will you be at the party tonight?"

They were celebrating Faith's birthday. All the ranch hands and a good number of the townsfolk had been invited. "I wouldn't miss it."

"See you then." With that, Berringer gave a nod toward Faith. "I have some things to show you over here."

"I'll join you in a minute." After he walked off, she tipped back her Stetson, met Rawley's gaze, and planted her hands on her hips. "I wouldn't be surprised to learn you'd brought that rattler here in a burlap sack and then released it so you could show off."

"I don't mess with rattlers. Ever." Not that her idea hadn't crossed his mind a time or two, but he wasn't going to risk a bite just to make a point.

"I don't know why you two always seem at odds."

Because of you. "I've got nothing against him personally."

She patted his leg, gave him another one of her disarming smiles. "That's good. Because I like him a lot."

Watching as she strutted toward the group sharing her plans, hopes, and dreams, he wondered if it was time to move on and find his own dreams.

Faith watched as Rawley urged his horse into a gallop and made quick work of putting distance between them. She didn't know anyone who sat a horse as well as he did—or was handier with a gun. She knew a lot of men used them as a decoration the same way a woman draped a necklace around her neck, but Rawley Cooper did not. He'd been working the range for too long to take any of it for granted, to think a danger might not suddenly appear.

She wore a gun as well, was almost as good a shot as Rawley, but Cole had never derided her for the addition to her wardrobe. It was just another example of the two men finding something about the other not to like.

"I think your brother was showing off with that little gunplay," Cole said.

Turning, she faced him. "He saved your hide and he's not my brother."

"I thought your family took him in."

"They did. But I just don't view him that way."

His eyes, a blue that reminded her of the sky first thing in the morning, narrowed. "How do you view him?"

"As a friend." Someone she trusted with all her heart. Someone who, of late, she was noticing in ways she hadn't before. When she'd turned to see him sitting astride his horse, it was as though her entire body had awoken from a long slumber. Her nerve endings felt more alive, her arms wanted to reach for him, and her legs wanted to wrap themselves around his narrow hips. But it was more than the physical awareness that wanted to shove itself to the foreground—all aspects of their relationship were deepening. Stretching out beneath the stars and talking late into the night with him brought more awe, riding over the range with him more pride. His smiles warmed more than they had before. His laughter lifted her heart higher.

"I'd like to be more than that," Cole said quietly, his hand discreetly reaching out and squeezing her fingers.

He was handsome in a polished sort of way, not at all rugged-looking like Rawley. But there was strength in him, too. And ambition. He saw where the future was going and wasn't going to be left behind. He filled her with excitement over the possibilities.

"It would take a brave man, Cole Berringer, to admit that to my father and face his scrutiny."

"Courage is not something I lack, Faith."

She'd told Rawley true. She did like Cole. She didn't know if what she felt for him would lead her down the path toward love, but she'd never been afraid to see where trails might lead.

She'd worn the damn red gown.

Leaning against the papered wall of the spacious parlor that was serving as a ballroom, sipping his whiskey, Rawley fought not to notice how creamy and smooth her bared shoulders appeared or how the low cut of the bodice revealed the upper swells of her breasts. With her midnight hair pinned up, curling tendrils left to whisper across her neck, red was the perfect shade for her—and she damn well knew it. She'd first worn the flowing gown at Christmas, and it had been difficult enough then not to acknowledge how she had evolved from a girl into a woman. Little wonder the men were circling her, vying for her attention, one after another leading her onto the dance floor.

The band made up of mostly fiddle players—led by Austin Leigh, whom no one could match when it came to pulling a bow over a violin—alternated a lively tune with a slower one. It was obvious most of the gents were timing their arrival at Faith's side so they were available for a waltz. In a way it was amusing to watch, but at the same time it irritated the devil out of him. None was good enough for her, but she flirted with them and gave them hope anyway.

Faith had taken after her mother in that regard. She found time for everyone: ranch hand, businessman, poor, wealthy—which was one of the reasons most of her dances were claimed. She had a way about her of making a man feel humbled by her attention.

He didn't know why he was still here, tormenting himself, watching Faith dance with one fellow after another,

Cole Berringer greedily making his way into the line every third or fourth dance. It was an unwritten rule among cowboys that a man limited himself to one twirl about the floor with a gal until everyone had a turn with her. In spite of all Dallas's efforts to get women out to this western part of Texas, men still vastly outnumbered females. But Berringer didn't pay attention to the rules, which in the end probably would take him far and ensure he kept the lady at his side happy. Rawley was pretty sure he intended for that lady to be Faith.

"Rawley Cooper. Just the man I was looking for," Maggie said as she waved a red bandana in front of him.

"Hello, Brat," he muttered with affection. "You're not heifer branding me." The term referred to the long-standing tradition of cowboys taking on the role of a female dance partner when women were scarce.

"But we have a lot more gents here than ladies. I need a few fellas to show their willingness to pretend to be the gal so more men have a chance to dance."

Having a handkerchief tied around an upper arm provided the signal that a fellow was willing to partner up with another man for a dance or two. Cowboys enjoyed dancing. "Nope. Look elsewhere."

She released a breath in irritation, then smiled at him. "You're no fun. I didn't even see you sneak in here."

"I didn't sneak." But he had to admit he hadn't drawn any attention, either. He'd never much liked being the center of anyone's focus, preferred hovering off to the side. Being noticed when he was a boy had earned him nothing but pain and humiliation. Walking the edge, staying to the shadows brought him a measure of peace.

"Are you going to dance with her?"

They both knew to whom she was referring. Maggie was his best friend, but sometimes she was downright irritating, especially when she managed to work things out about him that he wanted to keep secret. "I think she has enough partners."

"But you're her brother."

He grimaced as a tightness that would put any noose to shame seized his chest. "No, I'm not. I was raised by her parents, in their house, but that doesn't make me her brother."

"Exactly. So where's the harm in dancing with her?"

The harm was that he wasn't good enough for her, had done things that made him sick to his stomach if he recalled them with any measure of accuracy. Dallas Leigh knew the ugly details of his youth. Rawley would never forget the revulsion that had taken root on Dallas's face the moment he'd learned the truth about what Rawley had done. The man's expression had indicated he was on the verge of bringing up every meal he'd ever eaten. If Dallas ever learned Rawley had any tender regard for his daughter, the man who had given him a safe haven would send him packing—after he shot him dead. He took a slow sip of his whiskey. "You are the most aggravating female I know."

"But you love me anyway."

"I tolerate you, even if you're as pesky as a gnat but not quite as big."

She chuckled lightly. "I love you, Rawley."

"Maggie—"

"Your problem is you don't believe you're deserving of love, not even the kind one friend showers on another. I don't know what happened to you before you became part of this family, but I do recognize that you're one of the finest men I know."

Sadly, he looked at her. "You don't know many men then."

Her small fist made hard contact with his shoulder.

"Ouch!" He stepped back, cradling his whiskey. "You nearly made me spill the good stuff."

"I went to the university. I know plenty of men. I can also say with certainty that none are as stubborn as you."

"All your praise is going to my head, Maggie." Finishing off the whiskey, he set the glass aside on a nearby table. "Come on, I'll dance with you."

Before she could protest, he took her arm and led her onto the polished dance floor where people were whooping it up. With her, it was the quickest and easiest way to change the subject because once she got a notion in her head, she chased it with dogged determination. Besides, she was wrong. He didn't *believe* he was undeserving of love. He knew it as fact.

CHAPTER SIX

She'd known the moment he entered the ballroom. Like her father, he had a resounding presence about him. Even with his quiet ways, when he strode into a room, people knew. It was as though the very air they breathed came alive, the atmosphere charged. He rolled in like a welcome rainstorm.

"How did you get Rawley to dance with you?" Faith asked Maggie when she was able to catch a minute with her cousin later, after dancing with too many cowboys to count. The one she hadn't danced with, however, was the one she wanted to more than anything, but he had allowed his boot heels to brush over the dance floor for only a solitary tune. She'd waited her entire life to grow up enough that Rawley would stop treating her like a child. She figured nineteen meant she was on the threshold of womanhood. Maybe she'd even crossed over it after taking on the responsibility of expanding the Leigh enterprises into oil.

"I made him mad," Maggie said, handing Faith a glass of champagne.

Faith laughed with a measure of fondness edged with a bit of jealousy. "I've never understood y'all's relationship. You squabble more than any two people I know and yet you always remain friends."

Maggie sipped her champagne, curiosity keeping her gaze wandering over the people dancing and milling about. As a recently hired reporter for the *Leighton Leader*, the town's only newspaper, she was always looking for an interesting angle that might make a worthy story. "We've been getting on each other's last nerve for close to twenty years now, I reckon. There's never been any rancor between us. Just a tendency to try to out-irritate the other."

"Do you love him?"

That question had Maggie jerking her head around so quickly Faith was surprised she didn't make herself dizzy. "As a friend, nothing more. Besides, he's been madly in love with someone else for the longest and I can't compete with that."

Faith couldn't have been more surprised if her cousin had suddenly announced a cattle stampede inside the house. Any woman would be fortunate to hold Rawley's affections, but he'd never hinted that he had an ounce of interest in courting. "Who?"

Maggie simply shook her head and turned her attention back to the guests.

"Maggie, you can't just drop something like that on me and not give me the details." She glanced around. "Miss Tate, the schoolmarm?" She'd moved to town three years ago, was fairly young and pretty in a porcelain doll sort of way.

Maggie didn't react at all.

"How about Lydia Helmsley?" The butcher's daughter. She was short and stocky, gave a man plenty to hold on to, unlike Faith, who had always been too skinny as far as she was concerned. In school, boys had teased her that a good wind would blow her away. More than once, her mother had been forced to scold her about her unladylike behavior of throwing punches when someone said something she didn't like.

Maggie sighed. "If you'd pay any attention at all, you could probably figure it out."

She always paid attention to Rawley, especially lately. Everyone in town thought of him as her brother, even sometimes referred to him that way, but she'd never viewed him in those terms. He'd just always been Rawley, her friend, her protector, her aggravator. "Does she love him?"

"Not like he loves her."

"She's a fool then." Although even as she said it, she was struck in the area of her heart with a twinge that resembled jealousy. The notion of seeing him courting some spinster, of watching him holding her hand, sharing conversations with her, giving her half of his sarsaparilla stick, brought with it a physical ache. If he married, she'd see less of him. He might even move off the ranch, move into town. She couldn't imagine not sitting across from him during meals. It had been hard enough when he'd decided to live in a small cabin in the middle of a copse of mesquite trees a fair distance from the house. But he continued to join them for most meals.

"I have to agree with you there," Maggie said. "A fool *and* blind not to see she rules his heart."

"I've never even noticed him flirting with a gal."

"That's not Rawley's way. He's subtler than that."

Which couldn't be said for Cole. He'd been showering attention and compliments on her since he arrived, and she was struggling not to let it all go to her head. She'd never had a gentleman express interest in stepping out with her, mostly because men feared the wrath of her father.

Faith took a sip of the champagne. People had been bringing her glasses of it all night, and with each one she became more and more relaxed. Most of the town had been invited. Food was being served in the dining room while people wandered through the various parlors, visiting, and coming to the largest one to dance. Cards were being played in one room, billiards in another. If Rawley wouldn't dance with her, maybe he'd at least challenge her to a round of billiards. They were pretty evenly matched when it came to the game.

Then he was walking toward her with a loose-jointed swagger that had her mouth going dry. Or maybe it was the champagne. It didn't exactly quench her thirst. He'd donned his Sunday-go-to-meeting jacket over his crisp white shirt with a thinly knotted tie. His face was clean shaven, his thick hair—the shade of midnight—combed back. Once he was near enough to touch, he smiled. "Hey, birthday girl."

Girl. Why couldn't he have used the word *woman*?

He placed his hand on the small of her back, leaned in, and bussed a quick kiss over her cheek. She caught a whiff of the sandalwood cologne she'd given him last Christmas, but underneath it was the beloved fragrance of leather and horses and the wide-open plains. He'd always smelled of hard work and the freedom to do as he pleased. Her parents had put far fewer restrictions on his activities than they had on hers. Partly because he was older, but also because he was male, so they didn't worry about him as much. That difference had always annoyed her. A time would come when he'd be running the ranch—and it was something she could manage with equal success if given the chance. But she had her oil and knew she could make a name for herself with it. She had too much of her mother in her to fail.

"It took you long enough to get over here," she scolded.

"I didn't figure you'd notice with all the fellas buzzing around you."

Oh, she'd noticed.

"Think I'm going to call it a night," he added.

He might as well have smacked her upside the head. "The party's not over until midnight. We have a couple of hours to go."

"You're not wanting for attention, and killing that rattler today plumb tuckered me out."

By *attention*, she had a feeling he was referring to Cole's devotion. He'd waltzed with her three times, had her mother on the dance floor at the moment. "You have to dance with me before you go."

"I don't dance."

"You danced with Maggie."

He glared at Maggie, who merely raised her hands in surrender. "We didn't do it in secret." She playfully patted his shoulder. "You watch out for rattlers heading home. Although I suspect they will be far less dangerous than Faith if

you don't dance with her. I'm going to get some more champagne." She sashayed off.

"Why won't you dance with me?" Faith asked.

"You've got plenty of fellas anxious to take you on a turn
about the floor."

"But none of them are you." She hadn't meant for her tone
to be filled with such longing or wistfulness.

"Faith—"

"Why don't you like me?"

The shock on his face was rewarding. "You can't possibly
believe I don't like you just because I don't want to step on
your feet."

She slipped her arm through his. "You won't step on my
feet. Dance with me."

She felt his resistance give way as the stiffness left the muscles in his arm, as though he'd been bracing for this moment,
but now that it had arrived, found it not nearly as unpleasant
as he'd expected it to be. But when he started to escort her
onto the floor, she held him back. "Let's wait for the next one
to start. I want a complete dance." *And a slow one.*

For some reason, he'd been avoiding her of late, had been
finding one excuse after another not to be in her company, so
she wanted to make the most of the moments to come. She
knew her father had begun to give him more responsibilities
around the ranch, preparing him for taking over as foreman
as soon as their current foreman decided to hang his hat on
the peg for the last time and set aside his spurs, but Rawley's
noted absence seemed to encompass more than that. And she
found herself missing him.

He didn't argue with her. Probably because he didn't want to make a fuss and draw attention. He was like that, but it was difficult not to notice him. She'd never seen him be unkind to anyone, and yet he gave off a dangerous aura that signaled he was not a man to take lightly. Perhaps it was because his smiles were rare. Or the way his eyes scanned the world as though he was always searching for trouble, didn't quite trust what he was seeing as being the way things truly were. She figured Maggie knew more about him because she'd been around when Rawley joined the family. He'd been part of it by the time Faith made her appearance. Whenever she'd ask anyone why Rawley lived with them when her mother hadn't given birth to him, the answer was always the same, no matter who gave it: He needed a home.

A home. Not a house. As she'd gotten older, the distinction wasn't lost on her. But whatever had happened to him before he came to her family was long buried, and she suspected it was submerged deeply enough as to never make another appearance. She knew he had no other relations to speak of, no one to visit him or ask after him. She couldn't imagine not having all her aunts, uncles, and cousins about.

The music finally went quiet and a frisson of anticipation coursed through her, something she'd not experienced all night, not even with the first dance of the evening. Handsome cowboys, bankers, lawyers, store owners, and Cole—she'd taken the floor with a variety of men. Most of them young, unmarried, and yet with none of them had she counted the seconds until he took her in his arms.

But with Rawley she did, and when that moment came,

she knew what had been missing all these years—the absolute and untarnished knowledge that this man might be part of her family, but he wasn't family. She was drawn to him, and it most certainly was not as a sister to a brother.

As he led her into the waltz, he held a hand aloft so she could perch one of hers on it while his other hand barely landed between her shoulder blades, over the silk, and she wondered if he'd made a conscious effort not to touch her skin. Not all the men had. Her other hand came to rest on his shoulder, where firmness greeted her. Having seen him without a shirt numerous times, she knew without a doubt he was comprised of ropey sinew and toned muscle.

The intensity with which he watched her fairly had her breath catching. He certainly hadn't focused his gaze on Maggie in the same manner when he'd brought her out onto the dance floor. If anything, the entire time he'd given the impression he wanted to be somewhere else. She'd expected the same but instead was left with the sense he might be memorizing the moment.

"You look beautiful tonight," he said with such seriousness that anyone hearing him might have thought he was speaking to her for the final time, as one would to someone hovering on the precipice of death.

"Don't I always?" she teased, hoping to lighten his mood.

He flashed her a grin, released a huff of laughter. "You know you do."

"And you're handsome."

His smile was self-deprecating. "Now that the flattery is out of the way—"

"I mean it, Rawley. You're good-looking." His skin had a swarthiness to it from years in the saddle, mixed with his Shawnee heritage. His ebony hair fell over his brow, and her fingers itched to brush it back, to make it a little less wild, but nothing about Rawley had ever given the impression he was the least bit tame. "I could tell a lot of the girls were hoping you'd ask them to dance."

He just shook his head, never having been comfortable with praise. Her father didn't give it often, but when he did he meant it—and Rawley's cheeks would turn a deep hue of red. Faith had always thought he was adorable when he blushed, but she'd never teased him about it.

"Maggie told me that you love someone."

His eyes narrowed, a muscle ticked in his cheek, his jaw tightened. "That girl has got the biggest mouth—"

"If you'd tell me who she is, maybe I could help with your courting."

He gave her a pointed look. "What do you know about courting, Faith?"

That she had finally reached an age where her father would let gentlemen begin calling on her if they were willing to face the gauntlet of hard stares he was likely to bestow on them. "I know what ladies like. I could give you some tips."

"I don't need any tips. I can handle my own love life just fine."

"Is she here tonight?"

He flattened his lips, a sure sign he wasn't going to answer. How many times had he irritated her over the years by holding his silence on matters she wanted answered? Did boys like girls who climbed trees, rode horses better than they did, could lasso a calf, or could shoot a rifle with deadly accuracy? Although he hadn't kept silent on all the questions, he might as well have because his answer, "Just be yourself, Faith. You'll have them falling at your feet," wasn't a great deal of help when it came to figuring out what a fellow wanted.

Then they were no longer talking, simply moving in rhythm to the music. His gaze held hers, and she found herself falling into the dark brown depths of his eyes. No hint of humor resided within them. Instead he was all seriousness and something she couldn't quite decipher. But it drew her in, made her fingers clutch him where they had a hold of him. All the other couples faded away until it was only she and Rawley gliding over the floor in tandem.

For as long as she could remember, it had been like this between them. No reason to use words to communicate, always knowing what the other needed, wanted, was thinking. Only now what was stirring within her frightened her with its intensity, and yet she had the sense he was struggling against the same unsettling awareness.

As soon as the music went silent, he released his hold on her so fast that anyone watching would have thought she'd caught on fire.

"I need to get. Happy birthday, Faith."

She wondered why, when he walked out of the room, it was like he'd taken the light with him.

Chapter Seven

As the full moon slipped beneath the billowing black clouds, Rawley sat on his front porch in a straight-backed chair, the front legs raised so he was tipped back, and sipped his whiskey. Dancing with Faith had been a mistake. She was no longer a child. He could still feel the slenderness of her back against his palm. His nostrils had flared when he'd inhaled her scent—a muskiness intertwined with a sensuality—that was somehow different from what it had once been. As they'd moved in rhythm to the tune, he'd wanted to wrap those few curling tendrils bouncing along her neck around his finger and draw them gently toward him until her mouth was nearer to his—

Her lips had seemed redder, fuller, as though they, too, had matured in anticipation of a time when she'd be kissing men. And her eyes—sultry and knowing—had held his with such intensity that he'd wanted nothing more than to claim her as his. But she was still young, innocent, and naïve about men. Certainly she'd seen enough animals breeding to know the particulars regarding how it was done, but she didn't know all the subtleties of it, of how a man was different from a beast, how his hands would caress—

He shut that thought down like a corral gate slamming closed to pen up the horses.

After dancing with her, he couldn't stay and watch her waltzing about the room with other men, knowing what it was like to hold her in his arms. Seeing her with Berringer had been torment before he'd danced with her, but afterward it would have been pure misery. So he'd come back to his place and poured himself a whiskey, determined to forget— but all he'd been able to do was relive the moments over and over.

He'd danced with Maggie, who was as cute as a button, and hadn't given a single thought to putting his hands anywhere other than where they respectfully rested. When it came to Faith, though, his mind wandered to places it shouldn't.

And it seemed Faith was wandering as well.

Setting his whiskey aside, he let the front legs of the chair drop before pushing himself to his feet and walking to the edge of the porch to get a better look at her sitting astride her horse as it trotted toward him.

"Rawley!" she called out, extending his name so it had around five parts to it. She brought the gelding to a stop. "The party's over."

"What are you doing here, Faith?" he asked as he stepped off the porch.

"I wanted to see you. Help me down."

She was still in the gown, had been riding the horse astride, and the skirt had risen up to her knees, the moonlight glistening over her calves making his mouth water. She held her arms out toward him, started to list—

He rushed over and caught her as she was tumbling, stopped her from falling on her head. With her feet on the ground, she sagged against him.

"You're drunk," he said, wrapping an arm around her, holding her against his chest.

"A little. Lot of champagne." She shook her head, straightened, easing back until she stood on her own. A silly grin spread over her face as she whispered, "Cole kissed me."

The thought of that man lowering his lips to Faith's, of circling his arms around her, had him feeling strung tighter than a strand of barbed wire between two posts. Of their own accord, his hands balled into fists, and he decided he'd make use of them the next time he came within a foot of the arrogant oilman. "You don't know anything about Berringer. He took advantage—"

"No, he didn't. He's a gentleman. And I know lots about him. He comes from a good family near Houston. Pa hired some ex-Texas Ranger to look into him before he gave me the okay to work with him, before he'd give him permission to look for oil on our land."

As far as Rawley was concerned, none of that gave Berringer the right to know the taste of her. "You shouldn't give a man your favors unless you have an understanding between you."

"The understanding was that I wanted a kiss. Besides, I've kissed fellas before."

"Who?" The word came out a bark, harsh and echoing around them. "When?"

"John Byerly on my sixteenth birthday. Augustus Curtiss on my seventeenth. I always kiss some fella on my birthday."

Was her father aware of that? He'd tan her hide if he found out she was going around giving out something as precious as her lips puckered. "Why?"

"Curiosity. And on my sixteenth birthday I wanted to do something memorable. Guess I've been looking for that memorable ever since."

Had she found it? Probably not if she'd just been kissing boys and young men who'd never had the opportunity to ride a trail and pass through a cattle town where dance hall girls and soiled doves waited for their arrival. "Berringer give you that something memorable?"

He wanted to bite off his tongue for asking. He did not want to hear the man lauded for being an excellent kisser.

She studied him for a full minute. With his heart pounding, he waited for her to deliver a lashing to his heart with her confession that the oilman had given her exactly what she'd yearned for.

"Not quite," she finally said. "But maybe that's because he's not the one I had decided I wanted to kiss tonight." She pressed up against him, draped her arms over his shoulders, met his gaze straight on. "You are."

Perhaps it was because a little spark of jealousy had hit when she'd learned someone else had a claim to his heart. Or maybe it was because for the past couple of years, she'd compared every man who had crossed her path to him and found them all lacking in one regard or another.

They didn't share his love of the land that had been bred into her the moment she was born. They didn't respect the legacy that had been handed to them by those who had fought to free the territory so it could become part of the United States, or they didn't appreciate the sacrifices that had been made by those who had settled the land and worked to make it grander than it might have been otherwise. They boasted—instead of doing things in quiet ways that spoke volumes for them. Their smiles didn't slowly hitch up on one side before lifting up on the other. They didn't give her half a sarsaparilla stick. And they didn't stand so still that they might as well have been a statue.

"How much champagne *did* you have?"

"Are you afraid?" she taunted.

He scoffed. "Hardly."

"Maybe it's that you don't know how, that you've never kissed a gal before."

"I've done plenty of kissing."

"Then why not kiss me?"

"Because you deserve better."

"I'm not asking you to marry me, cowboy. Just kiss me." She gave her head a little shake, angled her chin up a tad, looked at the sky, the stars tossed over the black velvet. "On the other hand, could be I misjudged Cole's kiss, didn't give it enough credence. It did cause my toes to curl."

The only light came from the moon and stars shining down, yet she still managed to detect a tightening in his jaw.

"Those fellas you kissed before were just boys, and Berringer is a tenderfoot. I doubt they know the first thing about proper kissing."

"Then show me."

He emitted a low growl at the back of his throat as he cupped her cheek with one hand. "This is a bad idea, Faith. A damn bad idea."

Then he drew her in, lowered his mouth to hers, and urged her to part her lips. When she did, he claimed her mouth with the same intensity that a storm swept over the land, dark and billowing, giving no quarter, threatening to conquer all in its wake. The palm cradling her cheek moved until his fingers were threaded through her hair and his thumb was caressing the corner of her mouth, enhancing the sensuality of his efforts, causing molten warmth to slowly sluice through her, carrying her away on a tide of sensual indulgence. With his free arm snaking around her back, he pressed her flush against him, and she suspected that through his shirt he could feel the puckering of her nipples, their sensitivity increasing with each stroke of his tongue over hers.

His was not a timid kiss like those of the boys who'd come before. Nor was it civilized like Cole's. It was wild and untamed, a force to be reckoned with. It demanded a response equal in intensity. She wound her arms tightly around his neck because she needed purchase. Not only did her toes curl, but her legs had become as unsteady as those of a newborn foal, and she was afraid she was going to embarrass herself by sliding down the long, wondrous length of his hardened body until she was a heap of heated pleasure she'd never experienced, hadn't even known existed. With each passing moment, she was aware of a metamorphosis happening, as though he were weaving a cocoon around her, encasing her in ecstasy, and when the kiss came to an end, she'd emerge to discover she'd been transformed into something more beautiful than she'd ever thought possible.

He was doing things to her mouth that caused the womanly aspects of her that she thought had blossomed to really and truly unfurl into a glorious bloom that stole her breath. Within his arms, for the first time in her life, she felt power beneath her femininity, knew the full extent of the strength residing within her.

As she returned the kiss with identical fervor, she felt equal to the task of meeting him on the terms he was setting and daring enough to set a few of her own. She scraped her fingers along his scalp through his thick black hair. From far away, another world, she heard sighs and groans circling around them. Her body tightened with needs and yearnings that were frightening in their intensity, but at the same time beckoned with the promise of more. And she wanted to take all that was offered.

With a desperate moan, she pressed her hips against his, searching for something she thought only he could deliver.

Suddenly he broke off the kiss, cupped her shoulders, and set her away from him. "Happy birthday," he grumbled.

Then he walked off as though he hadn't just rearranged her heart and soul while upending everything she'd believed she understood about Rawley Cooper. She didn't know him at all.

CHAPTER EIGHT

Kissing her had been a damn stupid thing to do, almost as stupid as allowing her to goad him into doing it. He should have just brushed his lips over hers and laughed about it, but no. His competitive nature had taken hold, and he'd be damned if he was going to let Berringer give her a kiss more memorable than his.

So he'd poured need, longing, and yearning into the kiss that had nearly knocked his boots off. Sweet Lord, he felt like he'd been struck by lightning. And now he was pacing his porch, finishing off his whiskey, striving to wash away the taste of her. Champagne had darkened her flavor, and he thought he'd detected a hint of all the sarsaparilla sticks he'd shared with her over the years. Or maybe he was striving to find some evidence she was still a child, some aspect of her that would have him thinking of her once again as the little girl he'd always wanted to protect. But she sure as hell wasn't a kid any longer.

She was a grown woman, and when she'd pressed herself against his body, he'd felt every soft curve, hollow, line, and . . . those little hard nipples that had made him want to lower her bodice and lick. But he'd managed to find some semblance of self-preservation somewhere because he knew if her father ever found out, he'd put Rawley six feet under. But he couldn't help but believe that one of the nipples against his tongue would have been worth the journey.

He ached with a need to possess her that had him fairly trembling and terrified as hell that he wouldn't find the strength to never touch her again.

And he was going to have to touch her again to get her up into the saddle because the liquor had made her too unsteady to get herself up there. He didn't know how she'd managed it the first time. Then he'd have to escort her home. He halfway wanted her to say something. Instead she just stood there swaying slightly and watching him. He couldn't leave her out here, couldn't think of a way to tactfully get them both out of this mess.

"Rawley?" she whimpered, her voice sounding small, like that of a newborn kitten.

"What?"

"I think I'm going to be sick." She dropped to her knees and heaved.

He was at her side, rubbing her back, before the second round hit her. Then the absurdity of the situation struck him, and he couldn't help it. He laughed, boisterously, with an edge of relief and embarrassment. When she glared at him, he laughed again.

As she straightened, he pulled a handkerchief from his

pocket and wiped her lush, perfect, beautiful mouth. "My kiss wasn't that bad, was it, Faith?"

She gave him a halfhearted smile. "No, but I feel awful."

"You're gonna feel a lot worse in the morning. Come on, let's get you to bed."

"I don't think I can ride."

Apparently she'd developed a gift for understatement. Even if he sat behind her and kept her in the saddle, it would be a long, torturous journey for them both—her because of the illness she was experiencing and him because she'd be in his arms.

"You can sleep here."

He helped her to her feet. She'd taken two steps before she started to stumble. He swept her into his arms. With a little sigh, she nestled her head in the crook of his shoulder.

"I always thought I was too tall to be carried," she said pensively.

"It's all in the leverage."

"You're just strong. I've seen you bring a steer to its knees. Seen you do a lot of stuff."

"That's because you've been around for so long now. Nineteen is a lot of years."

He carried her into the cabin, into his bedroom, and laid her down on the bed. Her eyes were closed, and he figured she'd already fallen asleep. He started removing her shoes.

"Do you ever want more than this?" she asked wistfully.

Of course he wanted more. Like the ground thirsted for rain, and bees craved nectar. He longed to kiss her again until they were both breathless. He yearned to lay his body over hers and cause it to snap with relief when the tension was too tight, her cries of release echoing around him. "Go to sleep."

"You kiss good," she mumbled. "Better 'n Cole."

He grimaced. While her slurred words should have had him puffing out his chest with pride, he couldn't get past the fact that the kiss never should have happened—and she wouldn't be here if she hadn't had too much to drink. "About that. It shouldn't have happened, Faith."

"I know. 'Cuz of that lady you love. Tell me who she is, and I'll let her know you're a good kisser."

He set the shoes aside. "That's probably not a very good courting strategy."

"Are you courting her?"

"No."

"You should." She followed that comment with a little snore.

No, he shouldn't. He was too old for her. Too broken. And if he hadn't stopped that kiss when he had, he would have carried her in here and shown her exactly why he wasn't good enough for her. He wanted her with a need that scared the hell out of him.

Reaching across her, he grabbed the quilt and folded it over her. Then he stood there for the longest time just watching her sleep.

As the first hint of dawn eased through the windows, Rawley awoke, aching and sore, on the sofa. After stretching to work out the stiffness, he got to his feet and wandered over to the bedroom. Faith was still there, curled on her side, sleeping soundly. She was going to feel awful when she awoke, but he figured that wouldn't be for a few more hours yet.

He needed to let her parents know where she was before they discovered her missing and sent out a posse to hunt for her. He knew their routines, knew they were already stirring. Not bothering to take the time to wash up, he simply saddled his horse and headed over to the house.

Just as he'd expected, Dallas and Ma were sitting on the back veranda, where they always greeted the day. He pulled his horse to a halt, dismounted, and wrapped the reins around the railing before marching up the steps. They both rose, his mother approaching and giving him a kiss on his cheek as was her way.

"Good morning," she said.

"Morning."

"Looks like it's going to be a fine day," Dallas said.

Not for Faith. "I came over to let you know Faith is in my bed aslee—"

The punch to his jaw came quick and unexpected, sent him reeling back, stumbling down the steps until he landed in the dirt on his backside.

"Dallas!" Ma yelled, shoving the shoulder of the man who was now standing over him, fury darkening his features as he stood his ground, immobile against his wife's push.

"After all we've done for you, you take advantage of our daughter . . . Get up."

Rawley knew another punch was waiting at the end of those balled fists, closed so tightly the knuckles had gone white. He shook his head. "Nothing happened. She came to see me, was drunk, got sick, and I put her to bed. I didn't touch her." A bit of a lie, but if he confessed to kissing her, he'd be dead.

Breathing harshly, Dallas stared at him. A myriad of emotions—anger, betrayal, disappointment, regret, remorse—shifted over his features as his hands slowly unclenched. His resounding curse echoed around them as he bowed his head. This time when Ma shoved on him, he backed away three steps. She knelt beside Rawley. His hand shot up. "I'm all right."

He didn't want to be touched, not at the moment.

"I'm sorry, son," Dallas said, his voice coarsened by true repentance and shame.

"I'm not your son," Rawley said, pushing himself to his feet. "Your son is buried out by the windmill, and we all know that's because of me."

Because one winter night when he was a boy and a man had been rough with him in the alley outside the Grand Hotel, Rawley had cried out, and Cordelia Leigh, swelling with child, had heard him and come to his aid. The man, in a panic, had knocked a stack of crates onto her and injured her badly. She'd lost the baby she'd been carrying. If only Rawley had possessed the courage not to scream, not to draw attention to the horror he'd been facing.

"Rawley—"

"No. I know why you reacted like you did. I don't blame you. If I had a daughter and a man with my background touched her, I'd kill him."

"You weren't responsible for what happened to you."

"Still it happened." And it made him feel dirty and ashamed. All the baths in the world couldn't wash the memories away, couldn't make him feel clean.

"Let your ma tend to your lip."

Touching his tongue to the corner of his mouth, tasting the blood, he shook his head. "I have to leave."

The rightness of the words brought a calm. It was the only way he could make sure that what Dallas feared would happen between him and Faith never happened. "I have to leave here, make my own way, become my own man. I'll never be able to repay what you've done for me." But leaving was a start.

With a great gust of a sigh, Dallas dropped his head back and gazed at the pinkish-purplish haze of dawn. "I struck you in fear, fear that my daughter might have gotten hurt and there was nothing I could do to stop it."

"I'd never hurt her."

"I know that."

"We can talk this out," his mother said tenderly. "There's no reason for you to go."

But there was. "I've been thinking of moving on for some time. To figure out what I want and what my place in this world is."

Dallas nodded toward the horizon. "When I'm gone, half of this ranch is yours."

The words struck him hard on so many levels. The price he would pay to have the land was the loss of Dallas, and in spite of their present misunderstanding, he still loved the man with everything in him. The fact that it was coming to him by default. "If not for me, you'd be leaving it to your son."

Dallas faced him squarely. "You are my son."

Overcome with emotions, afraid he was going to do something unmanly like tear up, Rawley shook his head. "It should all go to Faith."

"There's plenty for her."

"I'm not going to take what rightfully belongs to your blood."

Dallas shook his head. "I spent twenty years trying to ensure you felt like family, and I managed to destroy it all with one quick jump to a conclusion and a punch. I'm going to regret that for the rest of my life."

"You've got nothing to regret. I appreciate everything you've done for me, but I have to find my own destiny, make my own way."

Dallas chuckled low. "My brothers felt the same. I tried to corral them in and map out their lives for them, but eventually they broke free. I reckon maybe you're right. It's time to be your own man, not a shadow of what I think you should be. Later, we'll go to the bank, get you some funds—"

"No." He needed to leave now while his jaw still ached, and he could vividly recall how it had felt to have Faith in his arms. "I've got enough money saved." And he wanted to do this on his own. "All I need is the horse, my saddle and gear."

The hardest part was saying good-bye to the woman he considered to be his mother. He hugged her tightly, not sure where he found the strength to let her go.

Blinking back tears, she patted his cheek. "You write to me often, let me know where you are and how you're doing."

"I will."

He stuck out his hand to Dallas, grateful when the man gave it a firm shake. "There will always be a place here for you."

"Appreciate it." He hesitated, then added, "There's no reason for Faith to know what happened this morning."

"How are you going to explain the swelling lip?"

"I'll handle it."

He returned to his cabin, grateful to find Faith still sleeping. Leaning against the doorjamb, he memorized every aspect of her. The tangled mess of her black hair spread across his pillow, the lithe length of her body curled on his bed. Her long limbs that he desperately wanted wrapped around him.

She looked so innocent in slumber, her thick, sooty lashes resting on her high cheekbones. The sun had bronzed her skin without leaving a single freckle behind. In his eyes, she was flawless.

He regretted he was going to miss the flare of her temper when she awoke to find him gone. She was the most beautiful when her passions ran high. But he didn't want to carry with him any bitter words that might arise between them, and if she shed any tears, he didn't know if he'd find it within himself to do what needed to be done. With a lonesome sigh he left her to her dreams.

After packing a few things in his saddlebags, he mounted his horse and headed west.

CHAPTER NINE

August 1909

"Uncle Rawley, do you have a dog?" Callie asked, around the piece of bacon she was nibbling.

Faith and her daughter had arrived in time for breakfast, and so far the meal had been as quiet as the one the night before—which meant not quiet at all.

"I used to," he said.

Her delicate brow pleated. "What happened to it?"

It had grown old and he'd had to put it down, one of the hardest things he'd ever done in his life, but did he tell her all that? Did she know about death?

"He went to play in heaven," Faith said, sparing him the torment of possibly breaking this child's heart.

"You should get another one."

The girl was as bossy as her mother. "Maybe someday I will when I'm a bit more settled."

"I like dogs." To prove her point, she gave the last bit of her bacon to the scruffy mutt. "Rufus sleeps with me."

"I bet that makes him happy."

She nodded. "Are you gonna play with me today?"

"I gotta work."

"Speaking of that," Faith said, "maybe we should have a little private meeting before the men gather so we can discuss how we want to handle things."

"You're in charge. Just tell me what to do."

As though suddenly lost, she looked at her father, then her mother, then swung her gaze back to him. "You were in charge of things before you left."

He shrugged. "And now you are."

She seemed surprised, but also pleased. He had little doubt she could handle all the responsibilities of managing the spread and all the men who worked for them. She'd spent a good bit of her youth out on the range with him and Dallas, roping calves for branding, moving steers from one pasture to another, mending fences, hauling hay. She knew the workings of the ranch as well as he did.

"I guess we'd better get to it," she said.

While she gave her daughter a hug and a few final words, he meandered outside where the cowboys had gathered. He shook the hands of the men he knew, introduced himself to those he didn't, noted the absence of a few familiar faces. A lot of changes had taken place since he left.

Then Faith wandered out. Denim pants looked better on her than on any man he knew, and he fought not to notice how her curves were a little more pronounced. The dress she'd worn last night had hidden a good deal. The clothes she wore now revealed everything, and not a single aspect of her wasn't pleasing to the eye. Making her way into the center of the group, she came to stand beside him.

"What assignments are you giving us, Rawley?" one of ranch hands called out.

"Faith will be doing that, Beau," he said loudly enough for all to hear.

"But you're in charge."

"Nope. I'm taking orders from Faith like the rest of you fellas."

"We all thought Faith was just filling in until you got back," Mike said.

"You thought wrong."

"If you have a problem with me giving orders," Faith said, "I can go ahead and give you what you're owed, and you can move on."

Mike shuffled his feet like he thought she might start shooting bullets at them and he needed to be prepared to sidestep them. "Just surprised is all."

"I'm not sure why," Faith said. "I've worked beside a lot of you since I was old enough to sit in a saddle."

Rawley clapped his hands together once. A couple of men jumped. "I think that's settled. If you'll tell me where you want me, I'll get right on it. I'm anxious to figure out what all has changed."

"Why don't you ride the perimeter, check the fencing? It'll give you a chance to look things over."

He winked at her. "Happy to, boss."

She gave him a ghost of a smile, which had his heart soaring, gave him hope they were on the precipice of reclaiming the friendship they'd once shared. Wending his way through the gathered men, he ambled over to his horse and mounted up, heard Faith's voice ring out as she issued orders. One of the things he'd always admired about her was her determination to do what needed to be done.

B y mid-afternoon, Faith had taken care of everything she needed to, was pleased with the work the men were doing, pleased with almost everything except the slight awkwardness that still hovered between Rawley and herself. Several of the men had crossed paths with him during the day and reported his approximate whereabouts to her. Urging her horse into a gentle canter toward the north end of the ranch, she was determined to ensure everything was right between them before this evening.

Her family members weren't big on gossiping about each other, but they did notice things—and worried when they sensed something wasn't quite right. Her relationship with him meant too much to her, and she didn't want it ruined because of unresolved issues from a long-ago night and feelings toward him that had begun to stir when she'd been much younger.

Not that finally finding him did anything to calm the anxiety, because the sight of him was awakening a stirring of desire she hadn't felt in a good long while. He was restringing a section of the barbed-wire fence. Based on the glistening of his bronzed back, he'd long ago tossed aside his shirt. His broad-brimmed hat provided the only shade for miles.

Drawing her horse to a halt a short distance away, she simply watched in mesmerized fascination at the way his corded muscles bunched and stretched with his efforts, the manner in which his Levi's pulled taut against his backside, outlined his thighs. He was all sinewy strength in motion, and she had the insane thought that if anyone ever made a moving picture of him at his labors, she'd gladly watch it for hours and never grow bored.

A thousand times she must have seen him without a shirt—washing up at the watering trough after a day in the saddle before coming inside to wash up properly, taking a dip in the nearby river where he'd taught her to swim when she was seven, and moments like this when it was simply too hot not to let nature's occasional breeze waft directly over one's skin. But never before had her mouth gone so dry, had she thought how pleasing it might be to take a lick of that salty flesh. She felt as though the champagne from that long-ago night was once again having its way with her, making her dizzy with a want for things she'd set aside, putting thoughts in her head that had no business visiting.

If she'd married Cole Berringer—or any man, for that matter—she'd have been settling, settling because she'd never been able to attract this man, to make him view her as anything other than a kid sister. It certainly hadn't helped her case that she'd been a silly girl with flights of fancy who'd never known hardship until it came calling without warning.

Her horse snorted. Rawley stilled his actions, glanced over his shoulder, and straightened.

"What are you doing out here? Checking up on me?"

he asked as he released his hold on the wire, dropped his hammer, and wandered over to the post where his shirt stirred in the slight wind. He grabbed his shirt and shrugged into it with a smooth motion that rivaled poetry in its simple beauty. It took everything within her not to shout at him to leave his clothing where it was, to let her feast a little longer on something that never should have been served up for her enjoyment.

At least he didn't bother fastening the buttons before snatching his canteen dangling from the post and taking several swallows of water, his throat muscles working, his Adam's apple sliding up and down with his efforts, causing an unusual fluttering in her stomach that traveled clear down to the seat of her saddle. What the hell was the matter with her? She'd seen plenty of men drink. It was necessary if one wanted to survive out here.

Frustrated with the unruly awareness bubbling to the surface, she abruptly dismounted and ambled over to him. "I wanted to thank you for the way you handled the situation with the men this morning, supporting me, not trying to take over."

"You earned it, stepping in when Dallas needed to let everything go."

"If you'd been here, he'd have handed everything off to you. Or you'd have just naturally filled his boots. He always saw you as eventually running things."

"But I wasn't here. And one day the ranch will be yours. The men might as well get used to you being in charge. Besides, I didn't want to have to explain another black eye." His voice carried a hint of teasing that had a good bit of the tension easing out of her.

"I didn't blacken your eye. Just bruised your cheek a little. Does it hurt?"

"Only when I smile."

Which he did at that moment, bestowing on her the type of inviting grin that had no doubt stolen a thousand hearts. "Rawley, with the family gathering tonight, I want to make sure everything is right between us."

He watched her a full minute before reaching into the pocket of his shirt, pulling out a sarsaparilla stick, breaking it in half, and holding a piece toward her. For a man such as he, of few words, his actions spoke volumes. With a smile, she took his offering and slipped it between her lips, aware of his gaze riveted to her actions. Drawing some comfort from that, she nodded toward the spool of wire. "Poachers?"

"Maybe," he said around his sarsaparilla stick. "Hard to tell. You might want to have the men do a head count on the herd. It could just be someone opposed to fencing. They cut close to a half mile of it."

"Why didn't you find some men to help fix it? As much as I appreciate what you did this morning, you don't need my permission to order the men about if you see something that needs to be addressed. Truth is, you have as much right to issue orders as I do."

He gave her a familiar grin that usually had her smiling back, but now it made her realize how masculine and confident he was. He knew himself, knew what he wanted. "I like the hard work of pitting myself against the wire."

Which she supposed was his acknowledgment he'd issue orders if he needed to. "You won't be finished before company arrives. Why don't you stretch it and I'll hammer it into the posts?"

They worked well together, but then they always had. He stretched the wire taut, wrapped it around a post, and held it tight, watching as she secured it with a few strategically placed U-shaped nails. Although she wanted things right between them, he wanted answers and figured the direction of the questions was likely to put her back up but was willing to risk it.

"I rode by that area you had set aside for drilling." He was aware of the hammer hitting the nail with a little more force, causing the post to vibrate. "It looks like someone set fire to those derricks they were building."

Stepping back, she met his gaze. "Like I said, I lost interest."

It seemed a drastic measure to take for a mere lack of enthusiasm. "Berringer have anything to do with that decision?"

"Yep."

"Is he Callie's father?"

Her mouth flattened, but she didn't look away, as though she was weighing how much to trust him. Finally, she nodded.

"I thought you liked him."

She gave him a sad smile. "I thought I did, too."

She strode over to the next post. Following her, frustration at the man for hurting her and letting her down getting to him, he yanked on the wire so hard he was surprised he didn't jerk the previous post out of the ground. "What happened?" he asked.

With a shrug, she positioned the nail and gave it a whack. "We just didn't work out."

He wanted the specific reasons but knew from the tone of her voice that they weren't coming anytime soon. "Does he know about Callie?"

Another nail positioned, another whack that nearly upended the post. "Things were over between us before I knew I was with child. He was long gone. If he hadn't been, I wouldn't have wanted to be saddled with him, so it was just as well he wasn't around."

He couldn't help but think the man had a right to know. Hell, he'd want to know if he had a young'un about, which he might mention once their relationship moved from tentative to sturdier. "It had to be hard, Faith, having a baby, not being married."

She smiled, the wistful beauty of it nearly breaking his heart. "When I started increasing, I stopped going into town. Ranch hands figured it out, of course. I'm sure some of them didn't keep it to themselves; rumors circulated through the area. A few days after Callie was born, when I was strong enough to get out of bed, Pa took us into town, introduced his granddaughter to every banker, shopkeeper, lawyer, newspaperman, widow, man, and woman around. So much love and pride were reflected in his voice. Rawley, I have never loved that man more than I did that day."

He could picture it—Dallas with his long stride, his

bigger-than-life ways, daring anyone to find fault with the babe in his arms or her mother. The town might now have a mayor and a town council, but Leighton still belonged to Dallas. His influence could not be measured. No one wanted to get on his bad side.

"You should have let me know, Faith."

"She wasn't your responsibility. You left here looking for something, Rawley. I didn't want you coming back until you found it."

The thing he'd been searching for was standing before him. He couldn't imagine the courage it had taken for her to risk the censure of the townsfolk. She could have gone to some other town or city where no one knew her and told them she was a widow. "Why'd you stay?"

"Because this is my home."

She wandered over to the next post and he followed, going through the same motions as before with the wire.

"Did you meet anyone while you were away?" she asked.

"Met a lot of people."

She pretended to conk him on the head with the hammer. "Anyone special. A lady."

"Nope."

She seemed to take great interest in ensuring the next nail was positioned perfectly. "That lady you loved, the one Maggie told me about, do you know if she's still in town?"

"She is."

At that, her eyes came up to his. "Did you write to her while you were away?"

"I should have but I didn't."

"Is she married?"

"Nope."

She gave him a saucy, challenging smile. "Maybe you'll get up the courage to call on her."

With that, she sashayed off to the next post.

It had never been about courage. It had always been about believing he didn't deserve her. And he hadn't, but maybe not for the reasons he'd assumed. Perhaps there had been a bit of fear in him, fear that his past would taint whatever they might have had together.

But when he considered the courage it had taken for her to remain in the area knowing people would judge her, his own concerns about being judged were insignificant.

The one thing he did know was that no one would ever love her as much as he did.

Chapter Ten

"Faith give you that black eye?"

Rawley had expected some comment about his bruised cheek but had thought it would come from Maggie, not her father. Houston gave him a knowing smirk, or at least the set of his mouth strongly resembled a smirk. Half his face had been scarred "on some godforsaken battlefield" when he was younger, and the rivulets of thick tissue tended to keep that portion of his face immobile so it was sometimes difficult to interpret his smiles. But there was no difficulty whatsoever when it came to reading Austin's broad grin. The man was downright and irritatingly amused.

"I might have accidentally run into her fist when I got off the train," he admitted.

Austin chuckled. "I heard tell she was fit to be tied when you hightailed it out of here without discussing the matter with her first."

"I had my reasons for leaving as I did."

"Whatever they were, we hope they're behind you now,"

Houston said. "We're glad to have you home." He was the peacemaker of the family, a quiet man of few words, but when he did speak, people tended to listen.

Taking a sip of whiskey, Rawley glanced around. Houston's wife and four daughters were there, as were Austin's wife, Loree, and their five sons. Callie had been fed and put to bed already. Faith was still getting dressed. After working on the fence, they'd returned to the house to get ready. When he sank into the tub of hot water, he'd imagined her doing the same thing in the room next to his, thought of the soapy linen caressing her skin, the water droplets raining down on her.

Repairing the fence together, talking, had helped to re-establish the bond between them, and he wasn't altogether certain that was a good thing, because now Faith Leigh was a woman to be reckoned with. Maturity had added to her allure, and he wasn't certain he had it within him to resist her this time, wasn't sure he wanted to any longer. A woman of her courage was the sort any man would welcome at his side. Now that she was older, the years separating them didn't seem as big a gap. He was no longer a man, she a girl. They were both adults.

"Dee shared those postcards you sent her," Houston said. "You did a lot of traveling."

"For a while. I was trying to figure out where to settle."

"And in the end, you came back here. Just like Austin. He traveled the world playing his violin for folks, but when it came right down to it, he didn't find anyplace he liked better."

"Not quite true," Austin said. "I didn't find any *people* I like better. There's something comforting about being in the bosom of your family." He looked around, motioned with his hand. "And I wanted my sons to grow up with this. You, Dallas, and I—we only had each other. Now look at us."

The room was filled with conversation, laughter, hugs, and smiles.

"What are y'all jawing about?" Dallas asked as he joined them.

"Family," Austin said. "And Rawley was about to tell us about cowboying in Wyoming."

"Cowboying is cowboying," Rawley said.

"Everything go all right out on the range today?" Dallas asked.

"Yep." He grinned at the man who had raised him. "Although Faith told me if you asked, that was supposed to be my answer no matter what trouble we ran into."

"Did you run into trouble?" His voice held worry and concern, and Rawley figured it was difficult to let go of something when you'd spent the better part of your life building it.

"Everything was fine. A bit of fence needed repairing, but nothing we couldn't handle."

"It drives me crazy to sit here all day not knowing exactly what's going on," he grumbled.

"It drives you crazy that you can't beat Callie at checkers," Faith said, slipping her arm through her father's.

She wasn't wearing the red dress, thank God. The pink froth tucked in at her waist, and the bodice wasn't cut low enough to reveal much of anything. Her shoulders weren't bare, but the sleeves were so small he wondered why the seamstress had bothered. Decked out as she was, she reminded him of a spun sugar concoction known as fairy floss that he'd tasted at the World's Fair in St. Louis. It had melted in his mouth, and he wondered if he could make her melt. He was certainly tempted to try.

"That little darling beat me five times," Dallas muttered.

Faith laughed. "She told me." She held out her hand, fingers splayed. "Five times!"

So she had been delayed because she'd spent some time visiting with her daughter. She was a good mother, and he reckoned she'd give the same love and attention to all her children. Not that he was surprised. She excelled at anything she tried, which made her decision to give up on the oil a bit confounding. He'd have bet money she'd have ensured it was a success simply to spite Berringer.

"Uncle Houston," she said, giving him a peck on the cheek. Then she released her hold on Dallas and moved around him to give Austin a kiss. "Uncle Austin."

"Doesn't Rawley get a kiss?" Austin asked, and her gaze slammed into Rawley's. "It might ease the hurt of that bruise you gave him."

Rawley was torn between laughing loudly, brushing it all off as a joke, and stepping nearer so she wouldn't have far to travel and could get to him sooner.

Her eyes never leaving Rawley's, she said, "I reckon since tonight is about welcoming him home, I ought to be a little forgiving and do it proper."

His heart was pounding so hard it was as though she were

issuing an invitation to her bed. What should have taken seconds seemed to take hours as she skirted around Austin and leaned in, a light-as-a-moonbeam brush of her lips glancing over his cheek. As brief and feathery as it was, it somehow seemed to have more power than the one they'd shared outside his cabin. Maybe because this time she wasn't drunk and he wasn't thinking she was too young or innocent for one such as he.

When she leaned back, she smiled, the type of smile one dear friend gave another when they were sharing something special. And in that smile, he saw the potential for happiness.

When he had the house built, her father had anticipated having a large family so the long, white-linen-covered table stretched the length of the room and provided ample room for everyone. Her father was seated at one end, her mother to his left, near his heart. Faith sat to his right. Rawley occupied the chair beside their mother.

Uncle Houston had taken the one at the other end, Aunt Amelia to his left, each flanked by two of their daughters. Uncle Austin and Aunt Loree sat on one side of the table with three of their sons, while the other two were across from them. Seeing all her cousins gathered in one spot was a bittersweet reminder that her parents had longed for more children, but an accident that caused her mother to lose her first child had made it difficult for her to conceive and had prevented their household from growing beyond Faith.

After the food was spread out and the wine was poured,

Faith lifted her glass. "I'd like to make a toast." She waited until she had everyone's attention and then looked at the man who she had little doubt was well on his way to once again becoming her best friend. "It's good to have you back, Rawley. I missed the sarsaparilla sticks."

His grin was small, a little playful, but something else reflected within it hinted at secrets shared. "I missed having someone to steal them from me."

Laughter echoed around the table, the loudest coming from her cousins, who had all at one time or another been the recipient of a portion of the sticks Rawley constantly carried around in his pocket.

She lifted her glass higher, and a rousing "Welcome home, Rawley" echoed through the room.

After everyone took a sip of wine, food was passed around and the buzz of conversation filled the air as people began catching up with one another, their busy lives preventing them from getting together as often as they'd like.

"Rawley, I'm thinking of doing a series of articles on your travels," Maggie said.

The intense manner with which Rawley cut into his beef told Faith he wasn't at all comfortable with that notion. "Why would anyone care to read about my travels?"

"I think it would be interesting. 'The Life of a Traveling Cowboy.'"

"It wasn't as glamorous as you might think."

"I don't want glamour. I'm looking for stories of real-life adventures."

Faith was just as interested in the details of his life during the time he was away. Neither his postcards nor his letters had revealed much about the particulars of his days and nights.

"It seems to me you ought to go on your own adventures and write about them," he said.

"That's what I've been telling her," Grant, Uncle Austin's eldest, said. "I'm going to Europe next year. You could travel with me, Maggie. See the wonders, experience them firsthand, and write articles that will put people right there beside you."

"It's not the sights I'm interested in. We're losing a way of life and need to get it recorded before it disappears altogether. There's a fella going around taking photographs of ranch hands working because he believes a time will come when we won't have cowboys."

"As long as people want meat," Pa said, "we'll have cowboys. Maybe not as many, but the cattle aren't going to walk themselves to the train."

Faith met Rawley's gaze, and she wondered if he recalled how Cole had questioned his relevance, how she had expected he'd run the ranch while she established an oil empire. Everything could change so quickly.

People broke off into their own separate conversations. Faith found it difficult not to keep her attention on Rawley, not to listen and glean information about his time away. His affection for those surrounding him was evident in the intensity with which he listened to them speaking—the same intent look that crossed his face when Callie spoke to him. He'd make a good father, but then he'd had a good example.

"Rawley, you got home just in time for the grand opening of the new theater," Uncle Austin said.

"What was wrong with the old theater?"

"This one is for moving pictures," Faith explained.

"We thought about simply converting the other theater," her mother told him. "But I believe we still have a need for plays, opera, and culture. So I wanted to keep the stage. Laurel is going to manage the new one. She says moving pictures are becoming quite popular." She looked down the length of the table. "Laurel, honey, do you want to tell Rawley about the theater?"

Uncle Houston's second oldest daughter perked up. She loved talking about the moving pictures. She'd seen one a few years earlier when she'd taken a trip to Pittsburgh and afterward had returned home to regal them all with tales about it. "The Nickelodeon—that's what we're calling it—officially opens Thursday. Have you seen a moving picture?"

"I once peered through a Kinetoscope and watched a man sneeze."

She laughed. "This is much better. It's a story more than a single action. And it's on a big screen, so you watch it with other people, sharing the experience, knowing those around you are just as enthralled. I'm excited we're bringing something so modern to Leighton. The entire family is planning to be there. I hope you can join us."

"I look forward to it," Rawley said.

Laurel smiled as though he'd just handed her the moon. Faith didn't blame her. He'd always been a favorite among the cousins.

He looked across the table at Faith. "I assume you're planning to go."

"I wouldn't miss it."

"**A**re you sure you won't stay?" her mother asked after everyone had left. "Callie is asleep, and your room is ready for you."

Faith considered it but figured she wouldn't sleep a wink knowing Rawley was just down the hall from her. It had been difficult enough bathing in a room near his, imagining him lowering that long, lean body of his into steaming water. "I hate to wake Callie, so if you don't mind I'll let her stay. And Rufus, too, if that's okay. In case she wakes up, she likes to have him near. It sounds awful, but I'd enjoy having the cabin to myself, experiencing a little quiet."

"We love having Callie stay so that's no problem."

"I'll escort you home," Rawley said.

"That's not—"

"It's already dark, Faith."

She rolled her eyes. "Fine."

When the horses were saddled and they had mounted, since Callie wasn't with them, she decided she was in the mood for a bit of adventure. "I'll race you."

Before he could agree, she urged her horse into a gallop and soon after heard the pounding of his stallion's hooves. She pressed her mount to go faster. The moon and a thousand stars provided enough light to guide them.

Out of the corner of her eye, she saw he was gaining on

her, his grin flashing in the night. A subtle rivalry had always existed between them, and she'd appreciated that he'd never felt a need to let her win, had always considered her a worthy competitor. Tonight she drew comfort from the competition, grateful to be easing back into doing something with him that was as natural as breathing.

He beat her by half a length, whooping as he brought his horse to a halt. Sweeping his hat from his head, he waited as she eased her horse over. "What'd I win?" he asked.

"Bragging rights."

He laughed, the deep timbre of his joy circling on the air and landing on her heart as gently as a butterfly on a petal. "I'll take it."

She dismounted. He followed suit and helped her see to her horse. When they were finished, she walked to the porch, placed her hands behind her, and leaned her back against the beam that supported the eaves of the cabin where tonight she'd sleep alone. Even though they'd built on an extra bedroom for Callie, Faith was always aware of her daughter's presence, imagined she could hear her breathing, noted the creak of the bed whenever she rolled over. Faith would often wake in the middle of the night and go stand in the doorway, watching as her blessing slept. "I guess you'll head into town for a bit of revelry now. It's not that late."

"Wasn't planning on it."

"What are you going to do?"

"I was thinking of going for a swim in the river. Want to come?"

She smiled, shook her head. "I can't remember the last time I went swimming."

"Sounds like it's been too long then. Grab a couple of quilts. I'll resaddle your horse."

"Don't be silly. We can walk."

"It goes against a cowboy's grain to walk. I've seen men mount their horses just to cross from one side of the street to the other."

"Which I have never understood. It's not that far. Give me a minute to change."

By the time she returned wearing pants, a shirt, and boots, with her hair braided, he was holding a lit lantern he'd obviously taken from the peg outside the front door. She handed him a bottle of whiskey and hugged the quilts close.

He lifted the whiskey. "A woman who knows the way to a man's heart."

That was a misstatement if she ever heard one, but rather than arguing about it, she simply set off at a brisk pace, the light from the lantern giving her confidence she wasn't going to run into an unexpected critter. "Speaking of being too lazy to walk—"

"I'm not lazy," he interrupted her. "But I don't see the point in using my legs when another set will work just as well."

"I like walking. There's a peacefulness to it. Have you seen these automobiles that Ford fella is making?"

"Rode in one once."

She stared at him. "You did not."

"Sure did."

"What was it like?"

"Rattled a lot. Nearly shook my teeth loose."

"Some fella came through in one a few months back. He said someday everyone will be driving one."

"I'll stick with my horse."

"Still, I've been thinking we need a place in Leighton that sells the gasoline that folks who aren't as closed-minded as you will need."

He chuckled low.

"What's so funny?"

"You are your father's daughter. Always trying to figure out what people need, what's going to bring them here, keep them here."

"With cattle no longer being driven to the slaughter yards, towns are fading away. I don't want Leighton to be one of them."

"Do you ever think about leaving?"

"No. If I left, I'd be like you. Eventually I'd come back."

"You could go away for a short while, just to see some of the sights."

She smiled over at him. "I have your postcards."

"It's not the same, Faith. Standing at the edge of the Grand Canyon . . . it just takes your breath. Everywhere I went, I'd see something and wish you were there to see it with me."

Knowing he'd thought about her while he was away touched her deeply. A part of her wished she'd been with him. When she'd awoken the morning after they'd kissed, in spite of her aching head and roiling stomach, she'd believed that something significant had changed between them, that more than their hearts had connected, that their souls had merged. She'd been filled with the promise of love and happiness. Until she'd discovered he was gone.

She'd been devastated by the news that he'd decided to move on, away from Leighton, away from her. Her pride had taken a blow, her heart a punch. He'd been a constant in her life—and he hadn't even bothered to say good-bye. She couldn't help but believe that her kissing him had prompted his departure. Hadn't he told her it never should have happened?

But Cole Berringer had been more than willing to kiss her, so she'd compounded the first mistake with a second one, welcoming his courting of her. He'd spoken with her father, and Dallas had given Cole permission to visit with her in a nonbusinesslike manner. In his arms, she'd thought she might be able to forget about Rawley Cooper—but he'd always been there at the back of her mind, at the edge of her heart.

She watched the lantern light bobbing along over the ground with his strides. "So you thought about me while you were gone?"

"Every day."

She'd thought about him nearly every minute. "Why didn't you write to me?"

"I don't know." Regret laced his voice. "To be honest, I don't even know any longer why I left."

A peacefulness settled over her to have Rawley at her side.

She was careful to keep enough distance between them that their hands wouldn't touch, but it seemed his path wasn't as straight as hers because every now and then his knuckles glided over hers, and a shiver of unexpected longing coursed through her. It had been ages since she'd found joy in the presence of a man, but it seemed natural to inhale Rawley's scent and draw comfort from it. She had an urge to bury her nose against the soft flesh at his neck, feel the bristles along the underside of his jaw scraping along her forehead, catching on her hair.

The silence eased in around them, and she drew comfort from that as well, from acknowledging that with him, the quiet void didn't need to be filled with forced conversation.

With a laugh, she quickened her pace. She could see the outline of the trees, hear the rush of the water. The river cut a serpentine path along the Leigh property. Farther down, her father had battled with her mother's family over the rights to the water. Peace had come with an arranged marriage, and love had soon followed. She never tired of listening to her parents' story. It had always given her hope that she'd find her own love. It had taken her a long while to understand everyone's story was different, and not all of them ended happily.

At the edge of the river, she dropped the quilts to the ground. "Who's going first?"

"Ladies always go first. Dallas taught me that."

"No peeking!" she called out as she hurried over to the bushes lining the bank.

"I'm a gentleman," he yelled back at her.

Strange, she thought as she began stripping down to her

chemise and drawers, that she was doing something she'd never expected to do again—be comfortable with very few clothes on in the presence of a man. They said time healed all wounds. Perhaps after six years, hers were finally starting to cease their festering.

Chapter Eleven

What the hell had he been thinking to suggest this? He heard the bushes rustling and fought hard not to think about exactly what was causing that swishing of cloth hitting foliage. Instead he contemplated how much work needed to be done and how he was going to stay out on the range tomorrow, repairing fencing and moving cattle to areas with more grass and water, until he was dog-tired, too bone-weary to even offer to escort Faith home.

He didn't know how it was possible that his feelings for her had deepened but they had. Watching her giving orders to the men and standing up to them had increased his respect and admiration for her. He'd fallen in love with a girl who had captured his heart because of her sweetness, but she had grown into a woman made of steel and spunk—but still the sweetness was there. He saw it when she interacted with her daughter, noticed it when she exhibited tenderness toward her parents. She was curious about the world but rooted to the land—the same land that spoke to something deep within his soul.

While traveling he'd worked a series of odd jobs, had always felt untethered until he took the foreman's position in Wyoming—but still something had been missing. And that something was here: Faith.

The splash of water yanked him out of his reveries. Setting the lantern on a nearby rock, he laid out the quilts so they'd be waiting for them when they emerged from the water. After loosening a couple of buttons, he pulled his shirt over his head. He removed his gun belt—he'd put it on before leaving the house, never comfortable being without it—and set it carefully at the corner of one of the quilts. His boots soon joined it.

He walked to the edge of the river, the water lapping at his toes. In one quick but smooth movement, he shucked his Levi's, tossed them onto a nearby bush, and dove into the flowing stream. When he burst through to the surface, Faith was only a few feet away, treading water. Most cowboys couldn't swim, but Dallas had made sure Rawley learned how. When taking cattle across a river, a man never knew if an errant steer or a sudden gush of rushing water might knock him from his horse. Heading north, Rawley had encountered riverbanks lined with crosses.

And of course anything Rawley could do, Faith was determined to match.

"I remember you were always wanting to come here for a swim," she said now.

"I never felt like I could get clean enough."

"You took baths nearly every day."

Every night before he went to bed he'd sink into a tub and

scrub at his skin, trying to scrape away the feeling of others touching him, men he hadn't wanted anywhere near him. "Lot of dirt gets lifted off the ground when you're working with cattle, and it's gotta go somewhere."

"I feel like that sometimes, like I'll never get clean," she said, so quietly he almost didn't hear her.

"You still use that fancy soap. I can smell it when you walk by me."

"Lavender. Milled soap from Paris. You used to hate it."

He loved the fragrance on her but had complained about it because it had been safer not to let her know all the things about her that he liked. "I'd end up smelling like petunias anytime you hugged me."

She laughed lightly. "Lavender and petunias are two different flowers, two different scents."

"Flowery. That's all that matters. Men aren't supposed to smell like flowers."

"They're not supposed to wear flowers on their hat, either, but Uncle Houston does."

A faded and frayed scrap of linen with flowers embroidered on it circled the crown of his Stetson, had for as long as Rawley could remember. "I think Amelia made it for him," he said.

"She did, except originally she sewed it so Pa could identify her at the train depot in Fort Worth. Sometimes I wonder how different things would be if he hadn't broken his leg and sent Uncle Houston to fetch her."

"Some way or other, I think it would have all ended the same."

She tilted her head to the side. "Do you believe in destiny?"

He shrugged. The river in this section wasn't that deep. If he touched his feet to the bottom, the water would swirl around him about mid-chest. "I don't know. But if I'd wandered into the general store five minutes earlier or later, my path might have never crossed with Ma's and I wouldn't be here now." It had been the first time he'd encountered Cordelia Leigh. Most people, including Faith, believed it had resulted in the Leighs eventually taking him. Few knew the true story of what had happened the night Cordelia Leigh lost her baby.

"Then I'd have never met you," Faith said.

She would have—if something like destiny really existed. Maybe he would have been a cowboy who wandered onto the ranch and got hired. Although if Dallas and Cordelia Leigh hadn't taken him in, he'd probably have died years earlier or been such a bitter, angry man no one would have been able to stomach having him around. "Someone else would have come along to aggravate you."

As though tired of the conversation, she went beneath the water, came back up, flicked away a few strands of hair that had come loose from her braid, and began swimming away from him. He'd wanted her to admit he didn't irritate her, that she enjoyed having him about. He wanted to hear her laugh. He hadn't heard an honest belly laugh from her since he'd returned. She was a mother, which brought responsibilities, had taken on the burden of running the ranch, which brought with it even more duties and obligations as well as accountability. The success of the ranch now rested on her shoulders. But she was in need of a little fun.

With long, sure strokes, he went in pursuit, easily catching up to her. He grabbed her waist, tugged her under—

The scream that rent the evening air sent chills racing up his spine. Her frantic kicking and punching had him immediately releasing his hold on her and darting back, away from her. But she continued to thrash about, yelling, "No! No! No!"

"Faith, it's just me. It's Rawley. I'm sorry, darling." He held out a hand imploringly. "I didn't mean to frighten you."

She went still, quiet, but he could see her trembling, a wildness in her eyes as though she were fighting to get her bearings.

"I'm going to come hold you."

Her hand shot up. "No. I'm sorry. I have to get out now. Please just stay there."

He heard the quaking in her voice, the quick rush of her breaths. "I'm going to swim back to where I left my pants. I'll fetch your clothes, too. Wrap yourself in both quilts."

She gave a jerky nod and began wading toward shore, while he headed upriver, climbed onto the bank, and drew his pants back on. Then he located her clothes and hurried back to where he'd spread the quilts. She was sitting on one of them, the other draped around her, the lantern brought in close to her.

"I'm sorry," she said, watching as he neared.

"Don't apologize for something that wasn't your fault." He dropped down beside her, grabbed the whiskey, opened the bottle, and held it toward her. "Take a swig of this. It'll help warm you." Even though the night was sultry, she seemed chilled. "I'm going to build a fire—"

"I don't need a fire."

"I do." A few minutes later he drew comfort from the crackling of the flames as they licked at the branches he'd gathered, took gratification from watching as she leaned toward the fire she'd claimed not to need. "Faith—"

"I just wasn't expecting you to grab me is all. It took me by surprise."

"It was more than that, Faith. We've tugged each other under the water a thousand times."

"We were children then. It's been years. I'd just forgotten is all. It's nothing. Let me have my clothes."

He handed the bundle to her, watched as she simply clutched it as though it was a shield of armor designed to protect her from all dangers. Only then did he notice she'd moved his gun so it was resting beside her hip, within easy reach. She might as well have lifted it and fired a bullet into his chest. It would have hurt less than the knowledge she felt a need to defend herself against him. "You know I'd never hurt you," he said quietly.

"I know."

So much was beginning to make sense. Her loss of interest in the possibility of oil that had once excited her. The burned beginnings of her dream. Her refusal to marry the man who had gotten her with child. "The same can't be said for Berringer, can it?"

Tears welled in her eyes as she held his gaze and shook her head.

"Tell me," he said gently.

"I can't."

He understood too well the difficulty of talking about something so incredibly horrendous and personal. "Okay, but I gotta get you warm. Take another sip of the whiskey."

Slowly, gingerly he moved around behind her, knelt, and began rubbing her arms through the quilt, creating friction and heat. She sighed, her muscles loosening as she began to relax.

"There's a falling star," he said to distract her. "Make a wish."

"I wish I could forget."

His heart nearly shattered with the sadness of her tone. "I know. But you can't."

She shook her head, then nodded as though confused by what her response should be. Settling down onto his backside, he brought her back against his chest and closed his arms around her.

"It's been so long since I've let anyone hold me," she said.

"If you don't want me to, I'll back away."

"No, it's nice. I can feel your warmth even through the quilt. It's better than the fire."

"You were always more skilled at building fires than I was."

She gave a little snort of laughter, settled into silence. He waited, just waited, loathing himself for not being here when she'd needed him.

"I liked him," she whispered in a raspy voice. "A lot. He charmed Ma and Pa. Charmed me. He was spending a lot of time at the house. Everyone figured eventually we'd tie the knot, that soon he'd ask Pa for my hand and his bless-ing. He'd gotten permission to take me to dinner in town. In the hotel dining room. You know how fancy it is, how eating there makes people feel special. Two bottles of wine later we were heading home, and I was so relaxed, so happy. He drove us out to the drilling site. We walked around for a while, talking about dreams. Then we started kissing. We'd kissed a few times before, but that night it was different. He wanted more, but I wasn't ready for that. But he wouldn't listen. He just took."

He tightened his arms around her, wanting to take away the painful memory, then loosened them, so she wouldn't feel threatened. He was searching for words, but all the ones in his vocabulary seemed far too insignificant to express how much he ached for her and what she'd suffered.

"He drove me home like nothing had happened, like he'd done nothing wrong."

"Did he go to prison?"

Her laugh was harsh, filled with pain and hurt. "I had no way to prove he forced himself on me. He was careful not to tear my clothes. Just shoved up my skirts. I had a few bruises where he held me down. Besides, they don't send men to prison for rape."

The harsh word—so small for an action so monstrous— was a kick to his gut.

"They would have argued I had loose morals or found some other excuse," she continued. "I often wear pants. How unladylike is that? To be honest, I'd rather face a charging steer than a courtroom full of people judging me with censure written all over their faces as I was forced to tell them the details of what happened. Only Ma and Pa know. The family believes I was susceptible to his charms and he took advantage. Everyone else thinks I was just naughty."

"But Berringer left."

She nodded. "Pa made him. I don't know exactly how. I didn't want to know. I just wanted him gone, and Pa said he'd take care of it."

Rawley figured Dallas had beaten the man to within an inch of his life—if he hadn't outright killed him.

"I'm sorry, Faith, sorry for what happened, sorry I wasn't here for you."

"You didn't know what Cole would do any more than I did. Still, I feel such a fool because I did fall for him."

"You're not a fool, Faith. Men like him are good at disguising what they are."

She twisted around slightly. "If he wanted me so badly—"

"It's not about want or desire. It's about control or dominance . . . or just downright meanness. Some people take pleasure in hurting others. I don't know why, but I do know what he did wasn't your fault." As he spoke the words, he was struck with how accurately they applied to him as well. He hadn't been to blame for what had happened to him all those years ago, any more than she was to blame for what had happened to her. Never before had he seen the truth of his circumstance so clearly.

Cradling her cheek, he held her shadowed gaze, saw the trail of tears glistening on her cheeks, gathered them up with soft strokes of his thumb. "Every time I think you're the strongest woman I know, you prove to be stronger than I realized."

"Knowing he touched me, I don't know how you can."

"Because he's nothing and you're everything." Taking his time, not wanting to spook her, he eased in until he could tenderly brush his lips over hers. She humbled him with her courage.

With a sigh, she snuck her arms around his neck and parted her lips, and he took what she offered as gently as he knew how, showing her with each restrained, slow stroke of his tongue, every caress along the length of her back, how precious she was to him. When she shuddered against him, he trailed his mouth along the creamy column of her throat, offering solace as she dropped her head back, giving him easier access. He followed a lazy path to the shell of her ear, outlined it with the tip of his tongue, felt the shiver course through her.

"Better than my birthday," she whispered.

Easing away, he held her gaze. "I want to offer you more, Faith, but I don't know if you're ready for it."

She shook her head. "But I'm getting there."

Straightening, she snuggled her back against his chest and he closed his arms around her. They sat in silence for long minutes, listening to the gurgling of the river, the chirping of the crickets, the croaking of the frogs.

"Are you going to leave again, Rawley?" she finally asked.

"Not if you don't want me to."

She merely nodded, and he knew in his heart he was there to stay.

She'd never planned to tell him, yet having told him, it was as though a great weight had been lifted. She didn't know how long they simply sat there, but it was comforting to have his arms around her, to feel his warmth surround her. Although it was August and hot, a coldness had seeped into her bones when the memories bombarded her, a coldness his kiss had obliterated. Unlike the one before, this one had been tame. Like the one before, it had him on a tight leash. She'd felt the tremors coursing through him as he held his needs at bay. He'd handed the reins over to her, allowing her to determine the depth, the direction, the pace their joined mouths would follow.

Eventually she slipped her pants, shirt, and boots on, wrapped a quilt around her shoulders, and they began walking toward the cabin. Without a word, he took her hand. She squeezed it as she brushed her shoulder against his. The familiarity of him was reassuring in its intensity.

When they reached the cabin, he said, "I don't want to leave, Faith. Memories were stirred up tonight, and I know how vivid they can be in sleep. I want to be here for you in case you have a nightmare, need comforting. I can bunk down in Callie's bed."

She'd never been all by herself through the night. Until she and Callie moved into the cabin, she'd lived in her parents' home. Always there was another presence. Although earlier she'd welcomed the peace, suddenly she didn't want to be alone. "I'd like that."

While he tended to his horse, she went inside, put away

the quilts and what was left of the whiskey. She wasn't drunk, far from it, but she was a little more relaxed.

When he walked inside, the entire place seemed to shrink with his presence. He filled the room, but not in an intimidating way. He was simply bold and confident, a man who could be tough one minute, gentle the next. She tilted her head toward Callie's room. With a nod, he strode into it. She followed and leaned against the doorjamb.

With a sigh, he bowed his head. If she had it within her at that moment, she would have laughed. Instead she simply smiled. Her daughter's bed wasn't much bigger than Callie was.

Without turning around, he glanced at Faith over his shoulder, a wry grin marking his features. "I reckon it'll be the sofa."

She bit her bottom lip, shook her head. "My bed."

He did turn then. "Faith—"

"Just hold me. I need that."

He nodded. "All right."

Her smile grew. Always a man of too few words.

Not bothering to change into her nightgown, she climbed into bed, curled on her side, and watched Rawley glancing around the room.

"You added curtains," he said unnecessarily.

"I didn't like the notion of someone peeking in." After Cole, she'd looked at the world differently, seen all the various ways she could feel violated.

He wandered over. The bed dipped with his weight as he sat and began tugging off his boots.

"It's hot. You can take off your shirt."

"You'll be comfortable with that?"

"I wouldn't have suggested it if I wouldn't be."

He pulled it over his head and tossed it to the foot of the bed. After lowering the flame in the lamp, leaving just enough light so they weren't in total darkness, he stretched out on the bed, raised an arm, and tucked a hand beneath his head. It was such a masculine pose.

Easing over, she snuggled against him, placing her head in the hollow of his shoulder. He brought his arm around her, holding her tenderly.

When she drifted off to sleep, she dreamed of him holding her like this every night for the remainder of her years.

CHAPTER TWELVE

"**D**id you kill Berringer?"

By the time Rawley and Faith got to the house, Dallas was in his office, looking over some papers. Faith had joined her mother and Callie for breakfast, but Rawley had needed a word with Dallas first.

The man who had raised him leaned back in his chair, planted his elbow on its arm, and stroked his forefinger along his mustache. "She told you."

Rawley gave a brusque nod and repeated his question. "Did you kill him?"

Dallas got up, walked to the marble-topped table, lifted a decanter, and poured whiskey into two glasses. In spite of the early hour, Rawley took the one Dallas offered him.

"He was still breathing when I left him. Barely." He downed the contents. "Don't think I wasn't tempted to put a bullet in him. Instead, I told him if I ever saw him in these parts again, I would. I let him ride out."

"Do you know where I'd find him?"

Dallas shook his head. "Even if I did, I wouldn't tell you. The last thing Faith and your ma need is to see you strung up for murder."

"I could do it without getting caught."

"You've never killed a man. I have. It's not something to be done lightly. I've put word out about the man. I get reports on him from time to time. He won't be courting anyone else's daughter."

That wasn't enough. If Rawley ever crossed paths with Berringer, he'd see to it the man drew his last breath.

He tossed back his whiskey, set the glass on the edge of the desk. "I love Faith."

Dallas stood still for a few seconds, then nodded. "I know."

"Not like a sister, not like a friend. I'm going to be where she needs me to be, and if that means I'm not sleeping in this house—to be honest, Dallas, it's none of your damn business. What happens between Faith and me is between Faith and me."

Another nod. "For what it's worth, I'd be damn proud to call you son-in-law."

"I don't know if it's going to come to that. I'm not quite sure how Faith feels about things or if it's something she wants, but regardless, no one is ever going to hurt her again."

Rawley had avoided courting or getting involved with anyone because his heart had belonged to Faith for the longest, but he'd always felt too broken for her. But now she was broken, too, and he was determined to see that she mended. If in the end, it took her away from him, carried her into someone else's arms, he'd find a way to survive. All that mattered was that she was well and happy.

So he asked his mother to let Callie stay another night, and he told Faith that when they were done for the day, he'd meet her at the cabin, that he had something special in mind. He made all the plans, was quite pleased with how they'd turned out.

The one thing he hadn't counted on was the rain that hit just before he got to the cabin.

She was not nervous. But there was a measure of anticipation thrumming through her as she stood in the open doorway, watched the rain pounding the ground, and listened as it hammered out a steady staccato beat on the roof. It had been years since she'd looked forward to spending time alone with a man—she didn't count last night because they'd been together as friends. She had a feeling tonight was going to be a little different. The way his eyes had warmed when he told her he was making plans for them—and that Callie would be staying with her mother—had caused her to smile for the remainder of the day.

While she'd found herself nervous around other men, hadn't wanted to be alone with them, she'd never had the same reaction when it came to Rawley—except when he'd taken her by surprise in the river. She couldn't deny a connection had always existed between them. It pleased her to know that tonight they would have some time alone together.

Still, she had expected him to arrive on his horse, not in the buggy. When he brought it to a halt, he darted around to the back, picked up a large wicker basket, and bounded up the steps.

His grin was wry, self-deprecating. "So much for my plans."

She smiled. "A picnic."

With a nod, he glanced over his shoulder. "I wasn't counting on Mother Nature spoiling things."

"We need the rain," she pointed out, trying not to sound too disappointed for herself and for him, for the trouble he'd gone to. "We can picnic inside."

"It won't be the same."

"It'll certainly be different from any other picnic I've ever had."

His eyes warmed. "That's what I was hoping for."

He carried the basket indoors, then took the time to unhitch the duo of horses and get them into a shelter. When he came back inside, she tossed a towel at him, watched as he scrubbed it through his drenched hair.

"You left some of your clothes behind if you want to get into something dry."

His brows lifted in surprise. "They're still here?"

She wasn't ready to confess that some nights she slept with a shirt he'd worn before he left because it still carried his scent—faint but noticeable. With a shrug, she said, "Bottom drawer of the bureau."

While he went into the bedroom, to avoid thinking about his removing his clothes, she busied herself getting things ready. She spread a quilt out on the floor and set the basket on it. Although it was near twilight, the thick clouds and heavy rain had blocked the sun as it dipped toward the horizon, darkened the sky. Preferring the dimness, she lit only one lamp, then opened the door to welcome in the outside. The porch eaves prevented the dampness from getting inside, but the scent of rain wafted in on a cool breeze.

She was gazing out when Rawley came up behind her and gingerly placed his hands on her waist. With a sigh, she leaned against him, reached back, and brought his arms around her, folding them over her chest just below her breasts. Lowering his head, he brushed his lips over her temple.

"I've always loved the rain," he said quietly.

I've always loved you, she thought.

Slowly he turned her around. "I'd planned to feed you first."

"I'm not hungry for food." She skimmed her hands up his chest, over his shoulders, around his neck. "But what I am hungry for . . ." Tears burned her eyes. "I don't know that I'm ready, that I can do it. I feel so dirty—and you know how grimy I am."

"Like I told you last night—it wasn't your fault, Faith. When I look at you, I don't see him. I see only you. I see a woman who endured something terrible and rose above it to become a wonderful mother, an extraordinary woman."

She shook her head. "You don't understand, Rawley. You can't know what it's like—"

"I do know, Faith. I don't know how old I was. I remember my two front teeth were missing the first time the man who called himself my pa sold me to a depraved bastard."

Chapter Thirteen

Her heart lurched, her stomach roiled, and the tightness closing in around her chest made it difficult to breathe. All the pain she'd been feeling for herself now shifted over to him. With one hand, she cradled his jaw. She couldn't find the words, all she could do was hold his gaze, while the tears rolled over onto her cheeks.

With his thumb, he captured her tears. "Don't cry, darling. It was a long time ago."

"But it never leaves you."

"No, it doesn't. But you don't have to let it own you, and for the longest time I did. I thought what happened to me made me unworthy, unworthy to love, unworthy to be loved. I thought those men left something ugly inside me—that it would touch others. That it would touch you." He circled his thumb around her cheek. "That night you came here, I wanted to do a hell of a lot more than kiss you. I wanted to lift you into my arms, carry you to my bed, and make love to you until dawn.

"If I'd told you what I was feeling, why I thought the kiss was a mistake, maybe things would have changed between us. I don't know. Maybe you'd have kicked Berringer out of your life that night, maybe you'd have never been hurt. I left, Faith, because I was afraid if you came to me again, I wouldn't have the strength to turn you away. And I believed with all my heart you deserved better than me."

He'd wanted her? His kiss had certainly made her feel desired, and yet—

She shook her head. "But what about that woman you love? The one Maggie told me about."

He smiled tenderly. "It was you, Faith. It's always been you."

More tears pooled over onto her cheeks. "Oh, Rawley."

He angled his head, lowered it slightly. "If you don't want what I'm offering, all you have to do is say stop."

Only she did want it, had always wanted it. When his lips touched hers, she opened her mouth to him, to this incredible, remarkable man who had always connected with her soul in ways no one else ever had. Why hadn't she trusted her own emotions, her own instincts, her own wants? Why had she doubted the strength of what she'd felt for him?

As he deepened the kiss, she poured all she was into the joining of their mouths and the sweep of her tongue over his. While she hadn't had any liquor, she was still feeling drunk and giddy. She didn't object when he placed his hands on her backside, when he pressed her against him, and she felt his need for her, hard and long, straining against his pants, pushing against her belly.

She wasn't frightened or repulsed as she'd feared she might be. She sensed the unleashed strength there but also felt it within herself. His desire for her caused his body's reaction. Not a desire to hurt or harm or dominate her. But a desire to share, to let her know she was his equal. Otherwise he wouldn't have given her the power to dictate the terms.

"Stop," she said against his mouth, and he went immediately still.

Breathing harshly, he pulled away, held her gaze.

"I want this, Rawley, I truly do. Inside I feel so dirty. All the baths in the world aren't going to clean what needs cleaning."

"I know. There were times when I nearly scrubbed myself raw." He looked past her. "You know when I feel cleanest, Faith? When I'm caught in a rainstorm." He tugged off his boots and socks, then knelt and removed her shoes. Straightening, he reached down and threaded his fingers through hers. "Trust me."

She did. With all her heart and soul. So with her hand nestled in his, she followed him out onto the porch, down the steps, and onto the grass where her daughter played.

The rain was heavy, but not the driving, stinging sort. It washed over her, sending rivulets down her face. She'd left her hair loose. Rawley plowed his hands into it and once again took her mouth, his passion all the more heated.

Pressing up against him, she took pleasure in his deep-throated growl, felt it vibrating through his chest. With one hand still tangled in her hair, he wrapped his other arm securely around her and lowered them both to the ground until he was flat on his back and she was straddling his hips.

Looking down on him, she met his smoldering gaze.

"You're in charge, Faith. Either show or tell me what you want. Do with me as you will."

Dropping her head back, she laughed as the rain pelted her, as the shackles that had claimed her for too long fell away. She had nothing to prove to this man, no expectations to be met. His love for her ripped away boundaries, left her as free as the wide-open plains.

She returned her attention to him. "If you don't like what I'm offering, all you have to do is tell me to stop."

He grinned devilishly. "Darling, when it comes to you, that word is never going to cross my lips. I won't object to anything you want to do to me."

His words emboldened her. She grabbed his shirt placket with both hands, one on either side, and ripped it asunder, sending buttons dancing through the air. His eyes darkened.

"You have an awfully fine chest, Mr. Cooper." She lowered her mouth to the hollow in its center and lapped at the rain that was gathering there, at the skin just beneath the shallow pool of rainwater. His growl competed with the thunder as he stiffened. More power to her, more dominance, more control. She licked her way over his ribs, one by one, then up his neck, until she was able to take his lobe between her teeth and give it a little nip. "Return the favor," she rasped.

"Christ, Faith."

When she straightened, she took his hands and placed them on either side of the buttons on her dress. She studied his face, the hunger there, the need, the desire not to hurt. "Do it," she ordered.

His formidable muscles that she had watched develop over the years made short work of ripping away the bodice and chemise until she was bared to him from the waist up. Reverently, tenderly, he palmed her breasts, gently squeezed. "Perfect."

Lifting himself up, he circled her nipple with his tongue, made an X over it, circled it again, then closed his heated mouth around it. She cried out at the pure pleasure of it. He gave the same attention to her other breast before again taking her mouth and delivering a blistering kiss that stole her ability to think or reason.

Passion and needs took over as their mouths and hands traveled over bare skin, plundered what was exposed, stealing treasured touches as sensations heightened. Pleasure pooled between her thighs, and she craved release.

With swift, greedy fingers, she unfastened his pants and set him free. He took hold of himself as she lifted her skirts, lifted herself before slowly sinking down, absorbing the wondrous glory of his filling her. Bracketing his hands on either side of her hips, he guided her motions as she rocked against him while the rain crashed down, drenching them, washing over them, cleansing.

Stroking her hands over his chest, she dropped her head back and rode him hard and fast, the pleasure building until it whipped through her and sent her flying into a great abyss where gratification reigned. Her cry echoed around them, circling his growl as he bucked beneath her and she felt his hot seed pouring into her.

Collapsing on top of him, she welcomed his arms closing

around her. She held him tightly as the storm had its way with them and peace floated around her, settled over her.

Rawley thought his courting style lacked a lot in the way of finesse but couldn't argue with the end result. As he sat in the bathtub of warm water with Faith's back nestled against his chest, he'd never felt so clean.

"When did you realize you loved me?" she asked.

"I always loved you. But you were seventeen, going on eighteen when I realized what I felt for you was starting to shift into territory it shouldn't."

"That's about the time I noticed you avoiding me, finding excuses not to be around me. I should have figured it out. I guess I was still trying to figure myself out."

He dropped his mouth to the nape of her neck. "You turned out just fine."

"What do we do now?" she asked.

"Dry off, go to bed, make love again."

She laughed. "I meant where do we go beyond that. I'd like to explore what we have here but don't want to rush into any sort of commitment."

"I understand that, Faith."

She twisted around until her hip was pressed against his cock, and it jumped to attention. "I don't want Callie to suspect something's happening between us. Or my parents." Rolling her eyes, she shook her head. "Or anyone. It's not that I'm ashamed of you, of us, but—"

"I know. We'll lose all our choices."

With a nod, she settled back against him, sending the water rolling over them. "Pa would make you marry me."

He didn't think she needed to know he'd already spoken with her father. He didn't want her to feel she had to travel this trail with him.

"I do like your idea, though, of drying off, going to bed, and making love again."

And that's exactly what they did.

CHAPTER FOURTEEN

When Faith woke up that morning, all she wanted to do was stay in bed with Rawley, but they had responsibilities. Besides, she'd been anxious to see Callie. She'd never gone that long without her. So they decided they'd act as though nothing had happened, and that evening they'd take Callie to the opening of the Nickelodeon.

But as she stood in the lobby of the movie theater with Callie clutching her hand while jumping about and Rawley discreetly holding Faith's other hand, she couldn't help but believe she was glowing with happiness and wasn't certain how anyone could miss it.

"This is quite the majestic building," Rawley said, glancing around at the gold and red wallpaper, the red plush carpet, the elaborately carved molding on the banisters of the twin winding staircases—currently roped off—that led to the balcony seating.

"You know Ma. She likes to give people experiences to

make them feel special. Callie, you remember the rule about tonight, don't you?"

Callie rolled her eyes. "No talking."

"That's right. This is a grown-up event, but you get to come because you're family."

"Rufus wanted to come."

"This isn't a place for dogs. He's waiting for you at home," Faith reminded her. Rawley had come by in the buggy to pick them up, was going to take them back home.

Laurel chose that moment to make her appearance, standing on the landing at the top of the stairs. She clapped her hands several times to try to get everyone's attention, but too much excitement filled the room for people to pay much notice.

Suddenly an ear-splitting whistle rent the air, causing everyone to glance around. "Quieten down!" Rawley yelled, and the crowd fell silent.

Laurel smiled. "Thank you, Cousin Rawley. Welcome, everyone! Aunt Dee, Uncle Dallas, and I are so happy you've joined us tonight. We think you're in for a unique experience. While moving pictures have been around for a few years, they are gaining in popularity. Theaters dedicated to showing them are being built around the country. As you know, my aunt and uncle think it's important we keep up with the changing times. So tonight we have for your enjoyment *Oliver Twist*. We also have the exceptional talents of Austin and Grant Leigh to provide the music that will accompany the film. You may sit on the main floor or we're removing the ropes, so you can come up to the balcony. Enjoy your journey into magic!"

People began wandering toward the doorways that led into the theater.

Reaching down, Rawley snatched Callie up into his arms. "We can't have you getting lost," he told her. He shifted her over so he could support her with one arm, then reached down and threaded his fingers through Faith's.

Yes, people were bound to notice she was glowing like a star-filled sky, but she couldn't help it. He made her feel treasured.

The crowd was meandering in, searching for empty seats. Rawley began leading her along the edge, past people who were arguing about where to sit until he came to a row with several empty seats near the front. She sashayed by him and took the third seat from the end. He started to put Callie in the middle one, but she clung to his neck like a monkey.

"No! Hold me," she demanded.

Giving Faith a wry smile, he slid into the seat beside her and settled Callie on his lap.

Faith grinned teasingly. "She does have you wrapped around her finger."

"No more so than her mother."

The lights were dimmed. The violins played. The moving picture began rolling.

She heard a crack, smelled the sarsaparilla, and without thought held out her hand. Rawley dropped a smaller than usual piece onto her palm. Glancing over, she saw that Callie was already sucking on her piece. With a wink, Rawley slipped his into his mouth. Looking at this man with her daughter tightened her heart.

The black and white images flickering on the screen mesmerized her, although not nearly as much as the man sitting beside her, who had reached over and once again taken her hand. She had about twenty minutes of just watching him inconspicuously before the film came to an end. But the entire time, the hairs on the nape of her neck bristled. Once she glanced around the room striving to determine who might be staring at her or what might be causing her unease but didn't see anything out of the ordinary.

As they made their way out of the theater, she studied her surroundings, the people moving about. Out of the corner of her eye, she saw someone familiar—

Turning her head quickly, she hoped to get a better view but lost sight of him. Still, he couldn't be who she thought he was, he couldn't be Cole. He wouldn't dare show his face around here and risk having to deal with her father—or with her, for that matter. She'd been too shocked and ashamed to confront him before, but if their paths ever crossed again, he'd discover she was no longer the girl she'd been. That she now possessed a toughness—

"What is it?" Rawley asked.

"I thought I saw—" She shook her head. It was just her imagination toying with her because she was no longer letting the man dominate her thoughts, because she was moving beyond him with Rawley. Maybe a part of her wanted him to see that he no longer held any sway over her. "Nothing. I didn't get a lot of sleep last night. I'm just tired."

"I reckon you'll get sleep tonight."

She looked at her daughter, nestled against his shoulder, and was tempted to send her home with her parents, but Callie was her responsibility. She and Rawley would just have to figure out a way to be together in a manner that didn't have her little one catching them alone together. "I imagine I will."

On the drive home, Callie sat in her lap, doing all the talking she hadn't done during the movie. Although she hadn't been able to read the dialogue cards, she'd been fascinated watching the actors moving about on the screen. And she had lots to share about it as though they hadn't seen it as well.

When they arrived at the cabin, Rawley walked her and Callie up the steps to the door. Rufus came around the corner to greet them. Faith opened the door, and the hound bounded in, Callie racing after him, which gave her a moment alone with Rawley.

"Thank you for being so good to her," she said.

"She's like her mother. Easy to love."

Dear Lord, she wished this man was her daughter's father.

"Mama!" Callie called out.

"I have to go," Faith told him.

He slipped his forefinger beneath her chin, tipped up her face, and brushed a kiss over her lips. "Dream of me."

Laughing, she watched as he strolled to the buggy, giving her a view of his fine broad shoulders. She was most definitely going to dream about him.

Faith was just drifting off into a light sleep when she heard the horse's nicker outside her bedroom window. Every nerve ending bolted awake as she shot up in bed, her heart pounding so hard she wouldn't have been surprised if whoever was outside heard it. Barely breathing, not moving another muscle, she listened intently. The huff of noise had been too close to be her horse, enclosed in the corral not too far from the cabin.

The sense of foreboding she'd experienced at the theater had stayed with her, so she'd left the flame in the lamp on the bedside table burning low, which made reaching for the gun resting beside it an easy matter. Her heart slowed and her breathing eased as her fingers closed around the cool ivory handle. Sliding out from between the sheets, she didn't make a sound when her bare feet landed on the rough braided rug. The curtains were thick enough that the person sneaking around outside wouldn't be able to catch even a glimpse of her shadow, wouldn't know a reckoning was making its way toward him.

She hadn't left any lamps burning in the front room. The curtains weren't as thick. Moonlight filtered through the fabric lighting her way. She looked in on Callie, grateful to see she and Rufus were snug and asleep in her bed. Quietly she pulled the door closed.

When she reached the front door, she pressed her ear against the wood and listened. Silence. Eerie. Thick. Heavy. Unnatural. Not even a cricket chirping. Then the barest of noises came to her, from across the room, near the kitchen window. Someone was moving around along the side of the cabin.

Slowly, she unlocked the door, released the latch, and eased the portal open. Enough moonlight existed to show nothing skittering about. Knowing the planks well, which ones creaked and which didn't, she stepped onto the porch in absolute silence.

A crackling as dry leaves were disturbed caught her attention. The horse made a quick snort. A man's low voice followed. No doubt trying to silence the beast. She found it odd he'd kept the animal with him if he was trying to sneak up on her, but it was quite possible the man was a bullet or two shy of having a loaded gun.

She crept along the porch, her back skimming along the wall of the house. When she got to the edge, she peered around the corner.

Definitely a horse. And a man. A man crouched down, spreading out a pallet. Slipping her finger off the trigger, she stepped down from the porch. "What the hell—"

Rawley jerked upward and spun around so fast that she might have laughed had he not also drawn his gun from his holster in a practiced move that demonstrated his quick reflexes and his deadly aim because it was now pointing at her. "Goddamn it, Faith! You know better than to sneak up on a man."

"And you know better than to be where you're not expected. I damn near filled you full of lead."

With a flourish that spun his gun around twice, he seated

it comfortably back in the leather holster. "I just decided to keep watch."

The sigh she released was filled with as much love as it was with frustration. "I appreciate that, but I can take care of myself."

"I don't doubt that for a minute, but I don't like the idea of you being out here alone." He grimaced. "I know Callie's here, but she's not going to be a good deal of help if there's trouble."

He narrowed his eyes, moved his head forward a tad as though trying to get a better look. "Are you wearing my shirt?"

"It smells like you," she said.

He grinned. "The real thing smells better."

"You're not going to go back to the house, are you?"

"Nope."

"You might as well come inside."

"You know what's going to happen if I do."

She gave him her sauciest smile. "If I'm lucky, you're going to take this shirt off me."

Chapter Fifteen

With a soft sigh and a moan, Faith burrowed more snugly against Rawley. She could get used to waking up each morning with his arms around her, his scent filling her nostrils.

"Morning," he said, his voice low and raspy, not quite as awake as other parts of his body.

Tilting her head back, she smiled at him. "Morning."

"I need to sneak out before Callie wakes up."

"She may already be up. I heard the front door—"

Rufus's barks filled the air.

She groaned, buried her face in the curve of his neck. "Yep. They're up."

"I don't suppose we have time to greet the day proper."

"I would like nothing better than to make love to you, but the fella who lived in this cabin before me didn't put a lock on the bedroom door. And Callie will just burst through because never before has there been a reason for her to knock."

"How are we going to explain my being here?"

Rufus barked louder.

"Let's hope she doesn't ask."

"Faith, she's going to ask." The barking grew in volume and intensity. "That girl is curious—"

More frantic barking.

"Something's wrong." Faith threw back the covers and scrambled out of the bed.

Rawley didn't question her. Just snatched up his pants, but she didn't wait on him. She drew her nightdress over her head because it was the quickest way to cover herself up. Not knowing what kind of critter had Rufus riled, she grabbed her pistol from the bedside table and ran. Her legs had never churned so fast.

The front door was open. She rushed through it, staggered to a stop.

A man was kneeling on one knee, his arm locked around Callie, holding her firmly between his legs. While she was struggling, it was obvious she couldn't break free.

"Mama!"

The man looked familiar but his nose was so misshapen— crooked and bent, nearly flat in the middle—that he hardly resembled the bastard who'd taken advantage of her.

"Let her go," she ordered.

Rawley stumbled to a stop at her back.

"Well, well, what have we here?" the man said, and his voice caused the short hairs on the nape of her neck to rise.

"Let her go, Cole."

"I don't think so." He waved a gun in his other hand then pointed it at Callie.

Faith swore her heart stopped.

"If either of you do anything stupid—"

"You're her father, Cole."

For the span of a heartbeat, he appeared stunned, then shook his head. "Doesn't matter."

"What do you want, Berringer?" Rawley asked pointedly.

"What do I want? I want my life back!"

He pointed the gun at Faith, and Rawley stepped in front of her quickly before she could even blink. He hadn't bothered to take the time to put on a shirt or his boots. Glancing down, she saw the gun he'd tucked into the waistband of his pants. She went to move around him, but his arm shot out, stopping her from going forward.

"And I want the damn dog to stop barking!"

"Rufus, play dead," Faith yelled. The dog whined. "Play dead," she ordered, and he rolled onto his side.

"That's impressive," Cole said.

"Grampa and me taught him," Callie said innocently, not truly understanding the dire danger she was in or that her life was at risk.

"Aren't you a clever girl?" Cole said.

"Let her go, Cole," Faith said. "We can sort this out."

"She's my leverage. I'd planned to use you, Faith. But he's"—he nodded toward Rawley—"been sticking to your side ever since he got back. Even cutting the wire couldn't separate you from Cooper. Then I saw you with this little tadpole last night—"

"You were at the theater," Faith stated with conviction.

"With it belonging to your family, I figured you'd be

there, that maybe I could get you alone. But once I saw her, I decided she'd be easier to handle. You've got too much fight in you, Faith. How does it feel, Cooper, knowing I had her first?"

She could see the tenseness in Rawley's muscles as he shrugged. "How does it feel knowing you've viewed your last sunrise?"

Cole laughed, a hideous sound. "A cowboy to the end, talking big. Except I'm holding all the cards."

"But like Faith said, she's your daughter. Once that sinks in you're not going to hurt her, no matter how much of a low-down skunk you are. Me, on the other hand—" Rawley stepped down from the porch and spread his arms wide. "I'm not armed. You let her go into the house and I'll drop to my knees right here. Then if your terms—whatever the hell they are—aren't met, killing me won't stop you from sleeping at night."

She was fairly certain that as soon as Callie was free, Rawley would be reaching for his gun—but with Cole's already drawn, Rawley's chances of hitting Cole before Rawley took a bullet weren't good. He had to know that.

"Ain't that the truth," Cole said.

Although he didn't release his hold on Callie, he seemed to be pondering his options, and Faith was thinking as well. Her gun was hidden in the folds of her nightdress. If he'd seen it, he would have ordered her to toss it. With him holding Callie as he was, she couldn't ensure she wouldn't hit her daughter. And even if she could hit him with unerring accuracy, did she want Callie to see a man shot before her eyes, to have his blood spraying over her? Did she want Callie to grow up with those images locked in her memory? If there was no other choice—

Cole finally nodded. "On your knees."

"Release her first," Rawley insisted.

"After you're on your knees. And put your hands up."

With little more than a glance back at her that reflected all the love he held for her—as though he knew it might be the final time he looked at her—Rawley did as ordered. Faith wanted to stop him but needed Callie out of danger. Everything within her wanted to scream, rant, and rave, but she held her silence as she continually evaluated the situation.

When Rawley's knees hit the dirt, Cole released Callie and gave her a little shove. "Go to your mama."

Callie raced to her, hugged her legs. Rufus saw that as his signal to no longer play dead and loped over to the steps. Without taking her eyes off Cole, Faith placed her hand on Callie's head. "Go into the house. Uncle Rawley's shirt is in my bedroom. There's a sarsaparilla stick in the pocket. It's yours. The whole thing." That would keep her occupied for a while. "I want you to stay in my bedroom with the door closed until Uncle Rawley or I come for you—no matter what you hear, you don't come out. Take Rufus with you."

"Come on, Rufus!" her little girl yelled before dashing into the house.

Faith heard a distant door slam shut and breathed a sigh of relief. For a little while her daughter was safe. "All right, Cole, now that you've got our attention, what is it you want?"

"Ten thousand dollars."

"I don't have ten thousand dollars."

"Your father does. You see what he did to my face? Beat it to a pulp. I can't even get a woman to look at me, much less fuck me."

Knowing her father, she had suspected he'd delivered a blow or two when he told her he'd taken care of Cole.

"Your lack of success with the ladies might have more to do with the way you treat them," she said, not bothering to tamp down her disgust for him.

"You were playing hard to get and always talking about him." He waved his gun at Rawley. "His stupid postcards, his letters, all the places he went, the things he saw."

"I didn't deserve what you did."

"I never had a woman complain."

Her stomach roiled. "I wasn't the first you forced?"

"You were the first to go to her daddy. Taking his fists to me and kicking me out of town wasn't enough for him. Somehow he managed to arrange it so I can't get any loans or any investors. Even my family won't help."

"He's a powerful man," Rawley said, "with a lot of influence in this state."

"Am I talking to you?" Then Cole jerked his attention back Faith. "I haven't been able to drill a single well since I left here. I'm ruined. So I want that money. You can go and get it, but if you bring anyone back here, he's dead."

"She's not getting you the money. She's not going anywhere. But you are. You're going straight to hell." Rawley lunged to the side, reaching back for his gun as he did so—

Cole fired. Faith screamed as Rawley went still. She rushed over to him, lifted his head into her lap, pressed her hand to his shoulder where the blood was oozing.

"You get him?" Rawley whispered.

She looked over at Cole. He barked out a laugh. "Looks like I'm just as good at killing rattlesnakes."

Then Cole's gaze went to his shirt where the red blossomed out. Blinking in disbelief, he stared at her. She'd been so worried about Rawley that she barely registered firing her Colt. His gun slipped from his fingers as though he no longer had control over them. Slowly he crumpled to the ground.

Faith turned her attention back to Rawley. "Yeah. I got him."

He grinned. "That's my girl."

"He could have killed you. I don't know what you were thinking," Faith said as she paced.

Rawley was sitting on the back veranda of her parents' house, his arm in a sling. She'd bandaged his shoulder as tightly as she could to stop the bleeding, helped him into a shirt, and tossed a quilt over Cole so Callie wouldn't see him. Her daughter had accepted Faith's tale that the man had decided to take a nap.

After Faith had saddled the horses, the three of them had ridden to the house so her mother could watch Callie. Then Faith took Rawley into town to see the doctor, while her father returned to the cabin with some ranch hands, got Cole into a wagon, and brought him to the sheriff. Once Rawley's shoulder was treated—the bullet had gone through, nothing vital had been hit—they'd both gone to the sheriff to explain what had happened, how she'd been forced to shoot Cole in self-defense.

Then they'd returned to the house, where her mother had convinced her they needed to stay the night. Her parents were keeping Callie occupied while Faith had it out with Rawley. She couldn't seem to stop shaking.

"I knew you had your gun," he told her now, "but you couldn't take advantage of that as long as he was using Callie for cover. I was hoping there was a spark of decency in him that would allow me to trade places with her. I knew you'd shoot him if he went for me, that you'd kill him and that you and Callie would be safe."

"But you didn't know if my bullet would stop him from killing you."

"Because I wasn't what mattered. When you told him that he was Callie's father, it hit me."

She came to an abrupt halt and stared at him. "What hit you?"

"That I loved her more than he ever could. It didn't matter that he'd planted the seed. Here"—he punched two fingers to the center of his chest—"in my heart, she's mine. If I had to, I'd lay down my life for her without hesitation or regret."

He stood, walked over to her, and wrapped his good arm around her, bringing her flush against him. "And I'd do the same for you. Nothing in this world is more important to me than you and your little girl. I'd like to make an honest woman out of you."

She gave him an impish grin. "Was that your idea of a proposal, Rawley Cooper?"

With a roll of his eyes, he started to lower himself to the ground. She stopped him. "Going to your knees once today was enough." She wound her arms around his neck. "I love you with everything I am. When I thought you were dead, the light in my world dimmed. I'll marry you on the condition you never put yourself in front of a gun again."

"From here on out, darling, we'll just lead a boring life."

"I beat Grampa at checkers!" Callie yelled as she skipped out of the house. "Again!"

"He's just not as good as you are, is he?" Faith asked.

"Uh-uh." She grabbed the beam and swayed back and forth. "Mama, you told that man he was my father."

With a deep breath, she released her hold on Rawley. She'd planned to have this discussion years from now. "I know. You see, Callie—"

"But he's not," she said in a tone that indicated there was no point in arguing the matter. "Uncle Rawley is."

"Why would you say that?"

"'Cuz I love him so much."

Rawley sat on the step. "I'd like to be your papa. Would it be okay if I married your mama? Then we could all live together."

Callie nodded. "Rufus, too?"

Rawley grinned. "Rufus, too."

Faith joined him on the step. Careful of his wound, she

circled her arms around him. "Do you think we might give Ma and Pa a few more grandchildren?"

"I'm certainly willing to give it my best."

Placing her hands behind his head, she brought him down for a kiss. She loved this man so much. She'd lost him once, didn't intend to ever lose him again.

Chapter Sixteen

One month later

"Maggie, how did you know Rawley loved me?" Faith asked her maid of honor as they stood in the large parlor drinking champagne, waiting as Uncle Austin and the fiddle players tuned their instruments. "Did he confide you in?"

"Hell no, he didn't tell me. I'm observant, figured it out on my own. The way he'd look at you—if a man gazed at me with such adoration, I'd marry him in a heartbeat." She shook her head, smiled wistfully. "But my God, Faith, when you walked into the room earlier, the way he'd looked at you in the past paled in comparison to what I saw in his eyes today . . . he was holding nothing back. Everyone could see how much he loves you. I wasn't the only one using a handkerchief to dab away tears."

Faith was wearing the same white gown her mother had worn on the day she married. Faith and Rawley had exchanged their vows in the same room where her parents had promised to have and to hold until death parted them, with the same preacher who had married them officiating. So many of the ranch hands and townsfolk came to witness the ceremony that chairs had been provided to only the family members so enough space remained to accommodate everyone else.

"He does have a way of looking at me that speaks volumes."

"About time you noticed," Maggie teased.

It was difficult not to when she could feel his heated glance across the room, when it conveyed everything he was feeling, promised a lifetime of happiness. He was standing between her aunts, occasionally nodding, but then his gaze would land on her and she'd feel the warmth of it as though he was nestled up against her. "I wonder what they're telling him."

Maggie looked over her shoulder, smiled. "Knowing my mother, they're probably dispensing words of wisdom regarding the little things he can do to let you know he appreciates you."

"He doesn't need any advice in that area."

The orchestra began playing "My Loree," a tune Uncle Austin had composed for his wife that reflected so many emotions, so much love that Faith teared up whenever she heard it. Catching her attention, Rawley tipped his head to the side.

Faith handed her champagne flute to her cousin. "Thanks, Maggie, thanks for being his friend and mine."

Then she strolled to the center of the dance floor where her husband waited. As soon as she reached him, with a warm smile and a flourish, he swept her over the polished wood in a waltz. People clapped, a couple of men whistled, but the man who had never wanted to be in the center of things didn't seem to mind that he had everyone's attention.

"If I'd known all I had to do was marry you to get you to willingly dance with me, I'd have done it long ago," she teased.

His laughter rang out deep and true. "You're going to be an easy wife to please."

"Were you dreading this moment?" she asked, because they'd known they'd start the first dance alone.

"How could I when it meant I'd finally have you back in my arms?"

Dear God, but she loved him.

People began wandering onto the dance floor. It was impossible to resist the lure of Uncle Austin's violin.

"What did the aunts tell you?" she asked.

"They thought I should take you to the Grand Hotel, so the night will be special."

"The night will be special because I'll be with you. Did you explain that we wanted to spend our wedding night in the cabin where we both became free?"

"I didn't think it was any of their business. I politely nodded and told them they were probably right."

She laughed lightly. "I doubt they were surprised by your brief answer. You have a reputation for not talking much, Rawley Cooper. Although they might be surprised by how much you talk to me."

"That's because you're my heart, Faith Cooper. And my

soul. When we get to that cabin, I'm going to give you my body, too."

Based on the heat warming her cheeks, she was fairly certain she was blushing. They hadn't been intimate since their encounter with Cole because they'd been staying with her parents. She'd needed some time to let the memories of what had transpired within the shadows of the cabin to fade. But it was where she wanted them to begin their life together tonight.

When the music drifted into silence, they separated but waited for her parents to join them. Then she waltzed with her father while Rawley circled the area with her mother.

"You look happy," her father said.

"I am. So happy."

"He's a good man."

"I think he had a good example."

He shook his head. "I'm a harder man than he is. War did that do me. Rawley had a harsh start in life but managed to hold on to his decency. With him looking out for you, I'll never have to worry about you or Callie. Or your mother. He'll take care of her, too."

Tears stung her eyes. "I love you, Pa. Please don't go any time soon."

"I'm not planning on it, sweetheart."

"Good. Because we intend to send a few more grandchildren your way."

His boisterous laughter filled the room. "I'm looking forward to that."

She had a need to catch sight of her husband, and when she did, her heart melted. He was no longer dancing with her mother, but with her daughter. Callie was standing on his polished boots, looking up at him, giggling as he glided her around the room. Faith sighed. "I love him so much, Pa."

"I doubt he could want for anything more, Faith."

But she intended to give him more, intended to give him everything she was.

The celebrating would continue for a few more hours yet, but Rawley was anxious to be alone with Faith—and everyone was graciously accepting of that fact. She was changing into something more suitable for traveling, even though they were only going to the cabin.

"We spend half our life waiting on women," Austin said.

"But the waiting is always worth it," Houston assured him.

"It sure didn't feel that way when I was waiting on you to bring Amelia from the train station in Fort Worth," Dallas grumbled.

"But it worked out for the best," Houston stated firmly.

"It did that," Dallas said.

It did indeed, Rawley thought. If not for the delay in Amelia's arrival, he might not now be watching the most beautiful woman he knew stroll into the room wearing that damn red gown that he couldn't wait to take off her.

"I'll see you around," he said distractedly to the three men who had first given him hope there was goodness in the world. As he headed toward Faith, he was vaguely aware of them chuckling behind him.

When he reached her, he didn't care that a horde of people remained in the room. He snaked his arm around her, brought her in close, and kissed her. "Ready, Mrs. Cooper?"

Her smile was bright enough to guide a cattle drive on a stormy night. "I am, Mr. Cooper."

He crouched down so he was eye-level with the little girl holding Faith's hand. "You remember the plans?"

Callie nodded with enthusiasm. "I'm gonna spend the night with Gramma and Grampa. Tomorrow we're gonna head to the Grand Canyon!"

He tweaked her nose. He and Faith had decided they were all deserving of a little trip together. "That's right. So you be a good girl, and we'll be over to get you bright and early in the morning."

Releasing her hold on her mother, she slung her arms around his neck. "I love you, Papa."

She'd taken to calling him that as the wedding neared, and it never failed to squeeze his heart. He enfolded her in his arms. "I love you, too, Little Bit."

He handed her off to her grandfather, who had followed him over, hugged his mother. Then he slipped his arm around Faith's waist and led her outside, the guests traipsing along behind them, calling out their good wishes.

After he hoisted Faith into the waiting buggy, she tossed her bouquet of wildflowers toward the crowd, laughing when Maggie caught it. He chuckled at the brat's shocked expression and couldn't help but hope someday soon she'd find a man worthy of her.

As Faith settled in beside him, he slapped the reins. "Giddyap."

The horses bolted forward.

Faith wound her arms around one of his and snuggled against him. Twilight was settling in.

"That dress drives me crazy," he muttered good-naturedly.

"It took me a while to figure that out. The first time I wore it you looked mad enough to spit nails." She pressed closer against him, gave his earlobe a little nip between her teeth. "Now I know it was because it made you want me so badly. I expect I'll wear it often in the future."

He chuckled low. "Fair warning. Whenever you do, it's not going to stay on you for very long."

They settled into silence, just letting the coming darkness wash over them. When they neared the cabin, she dug her fingers into his arm. She hadn't been back to the cabin since that fateful morning. He'd brought her and Callie's clothes to the house. He'd been the one to tidy up.

"It's not too late to go into town and get a room at the hotel," he said quietly.

Loosening her hold, she shook her head. "What I did is never going to leave me, Rawley. I don't feel victorious about it. But he didn't give me a choice. I believe that with all my heart."

"Because it's the truth."

She looked over at him. "We protect what's ours."

"With everything in us."

She nestled her head against his shoulder. "I have enough good memories of that cabin to chase away the bad."

He intended to give her more.

When they reached the cabin, he saw Pete sitting on the steps. With a wide grin splitting his face, the elderly cowboy came to his feet and approached as Rawley brought the buggy to a halt. "I didn't figure a newly married man would want to take time to see to his horses."

Rawley leaped from the buggy and shook the man's hand. "Thanks, Pete." Then he reached up, placed his hands on either side of Faith's waist, and brought her to the ground.

Leaning toward Pete, she brushed a quick kiss over his cheek, his face turning red enough to obliterate most of his fading freckles. "We appreciate it, Pete."

"My pleasure, ma'am."

Slipping his arm around her waist, Rawley led her to the cabin.

"That was sweet of him," she said.

"It was indeed."

As they neared the steps, he swept her into his arms, taking pleasure from the echo of her laughter.

When they reached the door, she shoved it open, and he carried her over the threshold, kicking the door closed behind them. He headed for the bedroom and didn't stop until they reached the bed, where he slowly lowered her feet to the floor and cupped her face between his hands. "I'm not a man of fancy words. I don't know how to tell you how much it means to me that you're my wife. All I can do is spend the rest of my life trying to show you—starting tonight."

With a smile that warmed her eyes, she brushed her fingers up into his hair. "I love you, Rawley, with everything that's in me."

His low growl reverberated around them just before he claimed her mouth, pouring all that he was into the kiss. With her he felt reborn, rising unscathed from the ashes of a dark past that no longer mattered. As she divested him of his jacket, vest, tie, and shirt, as each layer fell away, he felt the glory of her love washing over him. He was worthy of her caressing his skin. He was worthy of her.

"I love you." His declaration was ragged and raw as he leaned back and held her gaze. Her love humbled him, would have brought him to his knees if he didn't need to remain standing in order to remove the damn red gown that was keeping so much of her hidden from him.

He took care not to rip or tear it, yet still his hands worked swiftly until she was revealed in all her splendor. He tumbled them onto the bed.

"Your pants," she ordered.

One of the reasons he loved her was because she knew what she wanted and wasn't afraid to ask for it. He tugged off his boots, shucked off his pants, and stretched out beside her, his leg nestled between both of hers, his thigh pressed up against the heavenly spot that had been denied him for a month.

Lowering his head to the curve of her neck, he nibbled the soft skin, taking joy in her sigh, in her fingers digging into his back. Leaving a trail of kisses in his wake, he journeyed down to her breast, taking the nipple in his mouth, stroking his tongue over the little bud that came to attention for him.

She released a tiny mewl, lifting her hips and pressing her intimate core against his thigh. "I want you," she sighed. "I want you now."

"When I'm done worshipping you."

She didn't need to be worshipped, didn't need to feel like a goddess—she wanted only to feel like a woman, a woman desired, a woman loved.

No, she thought. She wanted to be a woman who desired, a woman who loved. And she did love and desire this man.

He wedged himself between her thighs, then scooted down and circled his tongue around her navel. Bending her legs, she pressed her soles to the backs of his firm thighs.

He pushed himself lower.

"Where are you going?" she asked.

Lifting his gaze, he fairly scalded her with the smoldering heat in his eyes. "Tonight I'm going to taste all of you."

Lower he went, spreading her legs, spreading her folds. When he lowered his mouth to the sensitive bud, she nearly came off the bed. Partly sitting, with her back curled, she rested back on her elbows and watched as he feasted.

"Oh, God," she moaned on a rush of breath as her entire body strained to be closer to him.

Acute sensations, forceful in their intensity, spiraled through her. With a groan, she dropped back on the bed and let them take over, as he worked the heart of her core over as though he intended to tame it. But he wasn't seeking to corral. He was seeking to free—

She screamed his name as her body spasmed, her back arched, and wave after wave of pleasure rolled through her.

Then he was there, buried deeply inside her, his mouth blanketing hers, as he pumped into her, hard and fast, until they were both crying out as ecstasy engulfed them.

When he went to roll off her, she held him close. "Not yet."

He sank down on her, levering himself on his arms to keep most of his weight off her, yet still she absorbed his warmth, his tremors. She welcomed the press of his lips against the curve of her shoulder.

"I love you, Faith," he said into the quiet.

She smiled. "How fortunate for me, since I love you, too."

And she would through all the days and nights that were to follow.

EPILOGUE

One year later

Faith sat on the porch swing beside her father, looking on tenderly as he cradled his month-old grandson, Jackson Cooper. It wasn't the first time he'd done so, but it always filled her with an abundance of happiness to see the joy and pride reflected in his face. He'd turned the management of the ranch entirely over to her and Rawley, who was standing with his backside pressed against the porch railing, his arms folded over his chest, one foot crossed in front of the other. Although she knew he wasn't nearly as relaxed as he appeared.

She also knew they made a great team with him handling the cattle while she had renewed her interest in oil. She believed with all her heart that before too long they'd find a gusher or two. But even if they didn't, she took comfort in knowing her father's faith in their ability to ensure his legacy continued relieved him of a burden he'd grown weary of carrying. And with any luck, he'd be with them for a good many more years.

Her mother sat in a nearby rocker keeping a watchful eye on Callie as she chased after Rufus, who would suddenly turn around and start chasing her. Her laughter and shouts of glee echoed around them.

"I can't believe how big this fella is already getting," her father said as he skimmed a roughened finger over what she knew to be an incredibly soft, chubby cheek.

"He's always hungry," Faith told him.

"He'll be eating beef before too long."

"I have little doubt," she assured him.

He lifted his gaze to her. "I would have loved him just as much if he'd turned out to be a girl."

She smiled tenderly. "I know, Pa. You never made me feel like you wished I'd been a boy."

"Not a lot of women could handle running a business as good as you do."

"I think you'd be surprised." She looked over at her mother. "We're pretty sturdy when it comes right down to it."

"We are that," Ma agreed.

"Your ma and I have been talking," Pa said. "We don't need this big monstrosity of a house anymore—"

"I never saw it as a monstrosity," her mother said quickly. "It represented a bold man with big dreams."

"Well, that bold man is growing tired, and you young'uns need the space more than we do, so we're going to build a smaller place not too far from here, but far enough away that you'll have your privacy. Or you can build yourself something else, but that little cabin just won't do any longer."

She glanced over at Rawley, and with nothing more than a quirk of his mouth, he told her his answer.

"We'd like to move in here," she said. "It's full of wonderful memories, and we'll pass them on to the children."

"Good, that's what we were hoping for," her father said.

"With that settled, are y'all ready for dinner?" her mother asked, starting to rise out of the rocker.

"Uh, before we do that," Rawley began, halting her progress, looking over at Faith. She gave her husband an encouraging nod. "Uh, I've got something to say."

Her mother lowered herself back to the cushioned seat and waited patiently.

Rawley straightened and slipped his hands into the back pockets of his pants. He shifted his feet, cleared his throat.

"What is it, boy?" her father asked, worry threaded through his voice, and she wondered if parents ever saw the children entrusted to their care as adults.

Placing her hand on his arm, she squeezed gently. "Just give him time." Then she gave her attention back to her husband and let all the love she felt for him—a lifetime's worth and beyond—reflect in her eyes. A corner of his mouth tilted up as he gave her a small nod before riveting his gaze on her father.

"Dallas, when I was a boy and you took me in, you offered to give me your name."

"And you turned me down."

"I didn't think I was deserving of it."

"That is such hogwa—"

She squeezed her father's arm to silence him because she

knew how difficult this moment was for Rawley, knew how very much it meant to him.

"Go on," her father said brusquely.

Rawley gave another nod. "I've been thinking on it. And the thing is, I want my son"—he looked to where Callie was now rolling on the grass with Rufus—"my *children*"—he looked at Faith—"*our* children to carry the name of my father. I was hoping that offer you made was still open and you'd give me the honor of taking on your name."

"'Bout damn time, son," her father said, his voice a little thready with emotion. "About damn time."

Then he handed Jackson off to her, shoved himself to his feet, and drew Rawley into his embrace. Over her father's shoulder, through the welling tears, she saw her husband's tightly closed eyes, saw a single droplet of water trail along his cheek.

He'd told her in the late hours of the night what he wanted to do, had asked her permission because it affected her name, too. He wanted to adopt Callie, as well, be as much a father to her as he would be to their son. And she knew he'd finally put his past behind him, had finally come to understand that family was not defined by blood.

"If it weren't Sunday, we'd head into town this minute and get the matter settled," her father said. "We'll do it first thing in the morning."

When her father stepped back, her mother replaced him, hugging Rawley tightly. "You've made us both so happy."

"It took me a while to see things right, to understand," he said. "Callie's as much mine as Jackson is."

As though she heard her name, Callie suddenly came to attention and darted up the steps. "Papa! I want a hug, too!"

Someday, Faith figured she would have to explain everything about the man who'd played a role in her existence. But her father was, and always would be, Rawley.

With the children sleeping, and their parents sitting on the front porch enjoying the stars, Rawley slipped his arm around Faith and led her away from the house, toward the open prairie. As far as he could see was land that would one day belong to them, that they would pass down to their children.

"Things change and yet they seem to remain the same," Faith said quietly.

"You'll be Faith Leigh again."

"I don't care what my name is as long as you're my husband."

He chuckled low. "Rawley Leigh doesn't exactly roll off the tongue."

"I like it." Swinging around, she stopped his progress, standing in front of him, her arms around his waist, her hands pressed to his back. "I love you, Rawley. I will as long as there is air to breathe and sky to look up at."

With one hand, he cradled her cheek. "I've loved you for so long, Faith, that I can't remember a time when I didn't."

As he claimed her mouth while the fireflies danced around them, he realized the legacy he'd been given had nothing at all to do with land or cattle or the possibility of oil but had everything to do with love, with loving this woman.

Chapter One

September 1876

His was not a face that women carried with them into their dreams.

Houston Leigh skimmed his thumb over the black eye patch before tugging the brim on the left side of his hat down lower. The right side showed little wear, but the crumpled left side carried the oil and sweat from the constant caress of his hand. Although the day was warm, he brought up the collar on his black duster.

Irritated with the world at large, his older brother in particular, Houston leaned against the wooden structure that had the dubious distinction of being Fort Worth's first railway station and gazed into the distance at the seemingly never-ending tracks.

He hated the railroad with a passion.

Fort Worth had been fading into obscurity, turning into a ghost town, before the citizens extended the town's boundaries so the railroad could reach its outermost edge. It had taken nothing more than a whispered promise to change the fading cow town into a thriving boomtown that the elected officials boasted would one day be known as the Queen of the Prairie.

The Queen of the Prairie.

Houston groaned. His brother had taken to calling his mail-order bride that very name, and Dallas had never even set eyes on the woman.

Hell, she could be the court jester for all Dallas knew, but he'd spent a good portion of his money—and his brothers' money—building this woman a palace at the far side of nowhere.

"We just need to get one woman out here and the rest will follow," Dallas had assured his brothers, a wide confident grin easing onto his darkly handsome face.

Only Houston didn't want women sashaying across the windswept prairie. Their soft smiles and gentle laughter had a way of making a man yearn for the simple dreams of his youth, dreams he'd abandoned to the harshness of reality.

Houston had known men who had been disfigured less. Men who had taken a rifle and ended their misery shortly after gazing into a mirror for the first time after they were wounded. Had he been a man of courage, he might have done the same. But if he had been a man of courage, he wouldn't have been left with a face that his older brother couldn't stomach.

He saw the faint wisp of smoke curling in the distance. Its anticipated presence lured people toward the depot the way water enticed a man crossing the desert. Turning slightly, Houston pressed his left shoulder against the new wood.

Damn Dallas, anyway, for making Houston leave his horses and come to this godforsaken place of women, children, and men too young to have fought in the War Between the States. If Houston hadn't been stunned speechless when Dallas had ordered him to come to Fort Worth to fetch his bride, he would have broken Dallas's other leg.

He still might when he got back to the ranch.

He heard the rumbling train's coarse whistle and shoved his sweating hands into his duster pockets. His rough fingers touched the soft material inside. Against his will, they searched for the delicate threads.

The woman had sent Dallas a long, narrow piece of white muslin decorated with finely stitched flowers that he was supposed to have wrapped around the crown of his hat so she could easily identify him.

Flowers, for God's sake.

A man didn't wear flowers on his hat. If he wore anything at all, he wore the dried-out scales of a rattlesnake that he'd killed and skinned himself, or a strip of leather that he'd tanned, or . . . or anything but daintily embroidered pink petals.

Houston was beginning to wonder if Dallas had broken his leg on purpose just to get out of wearing this silly scrap of cloth. It wouldn't do to anger the woman before she became his wife.

Well, Houston wasn't going to marry her so he could

anger her all he wanted, and he wasn't going to wrap flowers around the crown of his brown broad-brimmed hat.

No, ma'am. No, sir.

He hadn't stood firm on many things in his life, but by God, he was going to stand firm on this matter.

No goddamn flowers on his hat.

He squeezed his eye shut and thought about breaking Dallas's other leg. The idea's appeal grew as he heard more people arrive, their high-pitched voices grating on his nerves like a metal fork across a tin plate. A harsh whisper penetrated the cacophony of sound surrounding him.

"Dare you!"

"Double-dare you!"

The two voices fell into silence, and he could feel the boys' gazes boring into him. God, he wished he'd never shut his eye. It was harder to scare people off once they'd taken to staring at him.

"Looks like he's asleep."

"But he's standin'."

"My pa can sleep while he's sittin' in the saddle. Seen him do it once."

"So touch him and see."

A suffocating expectation filled the air with tension. Then the touch came. A quick jab just above his knee.

Damn! He'd hoped the boys were older, bigger, so he could grab one by the scruff of his shirt, hoist him to eye level, and scare the holy hell out of him. Only he knew a bigger boy wouldn't have jabbed him so low.

Reluctantly, Houston slowly opened his eye and glanced down. Two ragamuffins not much older than six stared up at him.

"Git," he growled.

"Heh, mister, you a train robber?" one asked. "Is that how come you're standin' over here so no one can see ya?"

"I said to git."

"How'd you lose your eye?" the other asked.

His eye? Houston had lost a good deal more than his eye. Trust boys to overlook the obvious. His younger brother had. Austin had never seemed to notice that his brother had left the better part of his face on some godforsaken battlefield.

"Git outta here," Houston ordered, deepening his voice.

Blinking, the boys studied him as though he were a ragged scarecrow standing in a cornfield.

With a quickness they obviously weren't expecting, he stomped his foot in their direction, leaned low, and pulled his lips back into a snarl. The boys' eyes grew as large as their hollering mouths just before they took off at a run. Watching their bare feet stir up the dry dirt in the street leading away from the depot, Houston wished he could run with them, but family obligations forced him to remain.

In resignation, he repositioned himself against the wall, slipped his hand inside the opening of his duster, and stroked the smooth handle of the Colt revolver. The thought of breaking Dallas's leg no longer held enough satisfaction.

Houston decided he'd shoot his brother when he got back to the ranch.

Amelia Carson had never been so terrified in all her nineteen years.

Afraid the train might hurtle her onto the platform before she was ready to disembark, she clung to her seat as the huffing beast lurched to a stop. The wheels squealed over the wobbly tracks, the whistle blew, and the bell clanged as the engine settled with an ominous hiss. The pungent smell of wood smoke worked its way into the compartment as the passengers flung open the doors, forgetting their manners as they shoved each other aside in their hurry to scramble off the train. Amelia had never seen such an odd collection of people crammed together in one space.

Women with throaty voices and low-necked bodices had graced the compartment. A few well-groomed men had worn tailored suits as though they'd been invited to dine with a queen. Only the guns bulging beneath their jackets indicated otherwise. Some men, smelling of sweat and tobacco, had squinted at her as though contemplating the idea of slitting her throat if she closed her eyes. So she'd rarely slept.

Instead, she had spent her time reading the letters that Dallas Leigh had written to her. She was certain the bold, strong handwriting was a reflection of the man who had responded to her advertisement indicating she had a desire to travel west and become a wife. He was a hero—inasmuch as the South could claim a hero in a war that it had lost. He had been a lieutenant at seventeen, a captain at nineteen. He owned his land, his cattle, and his destiny.

He had wrapped his proposal for marriage around dreams, dreams of building a ranching empire and having a son with whom to share them.

Amelia knew a great deal about dreams and how frightening it was to reach for them alone. Together she and Dallas Leigh could do more than reach for the dreams. They would hold them in the palm of their hands.

Countless times during her journey, she had envisioned Dallas Leigh waiting for her in Fort Worth, impatiently pacing the platform. Once the train arrived, he would crane his neck to see into the cars, anxious to find her. She had imagined him losing his patience and barging onto the train, yelling her name and knocking people out of the way, desperate to hold her within his arms.

With her dreams rekindled and her heart fluttering, she gazed out the window, hoping to catch sight of her future husband.

She saw many impatient men, but they were all rushing away from the train, yelling and shoving through the crowd, anxious to make their mark on the westernmost railhead. None wore her handiwork wrapped around the crown of his hat. None glanced at the train as though he cared who might still be on board.

She fought off her disappointment and turned away from the window. Perhaps he was simply being considerate, giving her time to compose herself after the arduous journey.

She pulled her carpetbag onto the bench beside her and opened it. With a shaky breath, she stared at the conglomeration of ribbons, flowers, and a stuffed brown bird that her betrothed had labeled a hat. Since she had no portrait to send him, he had sent her something to wear that he could identify.

She was grateful . . .

She stared at the hat.

She was grateful . . . grateful . . .

She furrowed her brow, searching for something about the hat for which she could be grateful. It wasn't an easy quest, but then nothing in her life had been easy since the war. Suddenly she smiled.

She was grateful Mr. Leigh had not met her in Georgia. She was grateful that she didn't have to place the hat on her head until this moment, that none of her fellow passengers had ever seen it.

She plucked it out of her bag, settled it on her head, and took a deep breath. Her future husband was waiting for her.

She just hoped none of the cowboys still mingling at the depot took a notion into their heads to shoot the bird off her hat before Mr. Leigh found her.

Standing, she stepped into the aisle, lifted her bag, and marched to the open doorway with all the determination she could muster. She smiled at the porter as he helped her descend the steps, and then she found herself standing on the wooden platform amid chaos.

Tightening her grip on the bag, she eased farther away from the train. She felt as though she were a shrub surrounded by mighty oak trees. She had little doubt that even the hat was not visible among all these men asking directions, exchanging money and paper with a purpose, and shouldering each other aside.

She considered calling out for Mr. Dallas Leigh, but she didn't think she could lift her voice above the horrendous yelling that surrounded her. She had expected Texas to be quiet and unsettled, not reminiscent of all the carpetbaggers who had come to stake a claim in the rebuilding of Georgia.

She shuddered as the blurred memories, images of Georgia during and after the war, rushed through her mind. With tremendous effort, she shoved them back into their dark corner where they couldn't touch her.

The men and women began to drift away. Amelia considered following them, but Mr. Leigh had written that he would meet her at the train station in Fort Worth. The sign on the wooden framed building proudly boasted "Fort Worth." She was certain she had arrived at the correct depot.

Slowly she turned, searching among the few remaining people for a man wearing a hat that bore her flowers. What if he had been here? What if he had seen her and found her lacking? Perhaps he had expected her to be prettier or made of sturdier stock. She had always been small of stature, but she was competent. If he'd give her the chance, she could prove that she was not afraid of hard, honest work.

She dropped her carpetbag and the platform rattled. Tears stung her eyes. She wanted so little. Just a place away from the memories, a place where the nightmares didn't dwell. She squeezed her eyes shut, trying to sort through her disappointment.

No man would send a woman tickets for a journey and

then not come to meet her. Somehow, she had already disappointed him . . . or a tragedy had befallen him, preventing his arrival.

People referred to portions of Texas as a frontier, a dangerous wilderness, a haven for outlaws. Newspaper accounts drifted through her mind. She latched onto one, and her imagination surged forward. Outlaws had ambushed him. On his way to Fort Worth, on his way to meet her, he had been brutally attacked, and now, his body riddled with bullets, her name on his lips, he was crawling across the sunbaked prairie—

"Miss Carson?"

Amelia's eyes flew open as the deep voice enveloped her like a warm blanket on an autumn evening. Through her tears, she saw the profile of a tall man wearing a long black coat. His very presence was strong enough to block out the afternoon sun.

She could tell little about his appearance except that he'd obviously bought a new hat in order to impress her. He wore it low so it cast a dark shadow over his face, a shadow that shimmered through her tears. Although he wasn't wearing her flowers on his hat, she was certain she was meeting her future husband.

Brushing the tears away from her eyes, she gave him a tremulous smile. "Mr. Leigh?"

"Yes, ma'am." Slowly, he pulled his hat from his head. The shadows retreated to reveal a strong, bold profile. His black hair curled over his collar. A strip of leather creased his forehead and circled his head.

Amelia had seen enough soldiers return from the war to recognize that he wore a patch over the eye she couldn't see. He had failed to mention in his letters that he had sacrificed a portion of his sight for the South.

His obvious discomfort caused an ache to settle within her heart. Anxious to reassure him that his loss mattered not at all, she stepped in front of him. With a tiny gasp, she caught her breath. She had expected the black eye patch. She was unprepared for the uneven scars that bordered it and trailed down his cheek like an unsightly frame of wax melting in the sun. With fresh tears welling in her eyes, she reached out to touch his marred flesh. His powerful hand grabbed her trembling fingers, halting their journey of comfort.

"I'm sorry," she whispered as she searched for words of reassurance. "I didn't know. You didn't mention . . . but it doesn't matter. Truly it doesn't. I'm so grateful—"

"I'm not Dallas," he said quietly as he released her hand. "I'm Houston. Dallas busted his leg and couldn't make the journey. He sent me to fetch you." He reached into his pocket and withdrew her embroidered cloth. "He sent this along so you'd know you'd be safe with me."

If his knuckles hadn't turned white as he held the linen, Amelia would have taken it from him. He had shifted his stance slightly so only his profile filled her vision.

A perfect profile.

"He mentioned you in his letters," she stammered. "He didn't say a great deal—"

"There's not much to tell." He settled his hat on his head. "If you'll show me where your other bags are, we can get goin'."

"I only have the one bag."

He leveled his brown-eyed gaze on her. "One bag?"

"Yes. You can't imagine how grateful I was every time we had to get off the train that I only had the one bag to worry over."

No, Houston couldn't imagine her being grateful for one bag. He allowed his gaze to wander slowly over her white bodice and black skirt, taking note of the worn fabric. Wouldn't a woman wear her best clothing when she met the man she was to marry?

Hell, he'd worn his best clothing, and he'd only come to fetch her.

He wrapped his fingers around the bag and lifted it off the ground. Judging by its weight, he figured she was hauling nothing but air, and they had plenty of that in West Texas.

She needed to be carrying all the things that they didn't have at the far side of nowhere. Hadn't Dallas told the woman anything about the ranch when he wrote her? Hadn't he told her they were miles from a town, from neighbors, from any conveniences?

Two bullets. He was going to fire two bullets into his brother.

"I'm ready to go," she said brightly, interrupting his thoughts.

No, she wasn't ready to go. Only he didn't know how to tell her without offending her. Without thinking, he removed his hat to wipe his brow. Her green eyes brightened, as though she were pleased with his gesture, as though she thought he'd done it for her benefit as a gentleman would. He fought the urge to jam his hat back on his head and explain the situation to her from beneath the shadows. "Did Dallas mention how long the journey would take?"

"He wrote that it was a far piece. I thought of a piece of cloth that I might use for quilting." She spread her hands apart slightly and her smooth-skinned cheeks flamed red. "But that's wrong, isn't it?"

Three bullets. He was going to shoot three bullets into his brother.

"It's at least three weeks by wagon."

She lowered her gaze, her eyelashes resting gently on her cheeks. They were golden and so delicate—not thick like his. He wondered if they'd be able to keep the West Texas dust out of her eyes.

"You must think I'm an idiot," she said quietly.

"I don't think that at all, but I need you to understand that this is the last town of any size you'll see. If there's anything you need, you need to purchase it before we leave."

"I have everything I need," she said.

"If there's anything you want—"

"I have everything," she assured him. "We can leave for the ranch whenever you're ready."

He'd been ready three hours ago, consciously packing and arranging all his supplies so he left half the wagon available for her belongings—only she didn't have any belongings. No boxes, no trunks, no bags. He cleared his throat. "I . . . I still need to pick up some supplies." He crammed his hat on his head, spun on his heel, and started walking. He heard the rapid patter of her feet and slowed the urgency of his stride.

"Excuse me, Mr. Leigh, but how did my fiancé break his leg?" she called from behind him in a voice sweeter than the memory he held of his mother's voice.

He turned to face her, and she came to a staggering stop, the bird on her hat bobbing like an apple in a bucket of water. Balling his free hand into a fist to prevent it from snatching off the bird, he wished now that he'd given Dallas his honest opinion on the damn thing when he'd asked him what he thought of it. "He fell off a horse."

Her delicate brows drew together. "As a rancher, surely he knows how to ride a horse."

"He can ride just fine. He took it into his head that he could break this rangy mustang, and it broke him instead." He spun back around, increasing the length of his stride. If Dallas had just listened to him, heeded Houston's warning, Houston would be back at his own place smelling the sweat of horses instead of the flowery scent of a woman, hearing the harsh snort of horses instead of a woman's gentle voice. He wouldn't have to watch a stupid bird nod. He wouldn't be carrying a bag, wondering what the hell she didn't have.

Four bullets. And even then he wasn't certain that thought could sustain him through the hell that tomorrow was sure to bring.

**And discover the rest of
the Leigh men in**

TEXAS GLORY

She never dreamed of the happiness . . .

Cordelia McQueen is little more than a prisoner in her father's house until he barters her off to a stranger in exchange for land and water rights. Now in a new place and married to a man as big and bold as untamed Texas, Cordelia prepares to live within her husband's shadow and help him achieve his goals.

Only he could promise her . . .

Dallas has one driving ambition: to put West Texas on the map. Convinced he's too harsh a man to be loved, he expects nothing except a son from his shy wife. But with each passing day, Dallas discovers a woman of immense hidden courage and fortitude. He is determined to give her his heart, even if it means letting her go to achieve her own dreams and find her own glory.

TEXAS SPLENDOR

A man on a mission . . .

After five grueling years in a Texas prison, Austin Leigh is finally a free man. He can't wait to go home and be reunited with his sweetheart. But when he discovers she didn't wait for him and is now married, he becomes more determined to clear his name of the crime he never committed.

Meets the one woman who could offer him salvation— and love . . .

En route to the state capital, he meets a young woman, Loree Grant, and her dog. When he learns that they have survived a mysterious tragedy, he is moved—and curious. And as he spends more time with the lovely, intriguing woman, he sees glimpses of a future he had thought was no longer possible as they both find a new lease on life—and a love that can overcome any obstacle . . .